Appearances

Appearances

Jan Seale

Beaumont, Texas

ISBN: 978-0-9852552-1-3
Library of Congress Control Number: 2012934315
Manufactured in the United States of America

Cover Painting: "Where have you been?" by Irene Hardwicke Olivieri
Cover Design: Erren Seale
Book Design: Sandra Chalyy

Lamar University Press
Beaumont, Texas

to storytellers everywhere

Acknowledgements

The author acknowledges with gratitude the initial publication of these stories as follows:

"An Adventure Is Made for Having," chosen for NEA/PEN Syndicated Fiction Project; also broadcast on NPR's "The Sound of Writing"

"After Long Silence," *Riversedge*

"Brush Boy," *Langdon Review of the Arts in Texas*

"Camp Knowledge," *Langdon Review of the Arts in Texas*

"At One Stride Comes the Dark," *Texas Short Fiction: A World in Itself, Vol. ii,* ALE Publishing

"Colors," *Compost Newsletter*

"Crossings," *Texas Short Stories 2,* Browder Springs Books

"The Day I Went to Visit My Innards," *Life on the Line,* Negative Capability Press

"The Halloween Alps Boys," *Passages North*

"How the Neighbors We Never Meet Move and Leave Us Lonesome," *Coe Review*

"It's Almost Sad," *Compost Newsletter*

"Loving Jerry," *If I Had My Life To Live Over I Would Pick More Daisies,* Papier-Mache Press; also performed in Boston Arts Theatre and Salado Living Room Theater

"My First Near-Death Experience," *The MacGuffin*

"The Noise Expert," *High Plains Literary Review*; also performed in "Arts and Letters Live" Texas Bound Series, Dallas Museum of Art

"The Only Dancing Dog in Captivity," *Red Boots and Attitude,* Eakin Press

"Ruling Passions," *Concho River Review*

"Take Cover," *RE:AL*

"Wheels," *New Texas '99*

CONTENTS

I. An Adventure is Made for Having

II. Some of My Best Friends are Relatives

III. Appearances

I. An Adventure is Made for Having

Loving Jerry

I have been wondering since the second grade what it feels like to fall in love. Then I get the note on Monday: "MEET ME AT RECESS BY THE WATER FOUNTING."

Jerry McCondle is one of the few people, boys or girls, in the whole fourth grade that fills up his T-shirt. (My mother says, "Nelda, you are s-o-o-o-o scrawny," when she pins me into a dress she is sewing for me.)

The other boys have sharp, bony shoulders and their T-shirts hang on them in wrinkles, showing their mothers have not flapped their shirts before they hung them on the clothesline. (One time when my mother made me wear a shirt a little bit wrinkled, I cried. She said, "Nelda, only real pretty girls have to have every little thing perfect.")

Anyway, Jerry's shirt even looks bulgy. And his jeans make a soft, swishing sound when he comes up the aisle.

He drops the little triangle-folded note in my lap as he comes back from collecting last Friday's spelling test. I leave it there and take off my glasses, holding them up like I'm wondering if they need cleaning. If I hold them a certain way, they are like a mirror and I can see Jerry behind me wadding his spelling test into a little ball and chucking it into his inkwell.

At the fountain, Jerry is careful to be five people ahead of me. He waits beside the water, saying things to each kid in line, sometimes slapping the water up into a person's face, especially if they are

1

wearing glasses.

When my turn comes, I try to wipe my mouth before I raise my head, but the icy water makes my lips numb and I can't tell whether I've gotten them dry when I raise up. In a way, I hope I haven't. The models in my mother's magazines all have wet lips.

"Hi," I say, feeling silly because I've been in the same room with him all morning. He doesn't splash my glasses and that makes me wonder if he is in love with me. He turns and walks beside me, not saying a word, just looking out at the baseball diamond where Rosemary and John are choosing their teams.

We stop behind the backstop. "We're going to sit there," he says, pointing to the old bleachers.

When we are settled, Jerry holds out his arm. On the inside is a big blue heart looking a little like the beautiful tattoo my Uncle Charles came home from the war with. It could be from the blue pen we have to use for English. The arrow could be from our red arithmetic correction pen. How would I know?

"Nelda," Jerry says slowly, "on Friday I'm going to have them put a girl's name in this. On Friday."

"That's nice," I say, staring out on the field where nothing much is going on yet. I figure I should probably know who "them" is.

When we go back inside, the health lesson is on the alimentary canal and my best friend Maydean and I glance through the chapter and count "body" four times and "bowel" twice. (Maydean has been in love I don't know how many times since last year when she moved to our school.)

Of course, the teacher calls on me to read aloud. She always calls on me.

One of my paragraphs says "body" and it makes me so nervous I start grinning when I get to that line and by the time I get to the word, I laugh out loud, put my hand over my mouth, and start coughing. Across the aisle, Maydean clamps her hand over her mouth too.

Miss Schumaker stands and stares at us. "May I ask what is so funny?"

2

I shake my head and continue to cough. There is no way to tell Miss Schumaker that Maydean and I *know* that "body" is a nasty word.

Tuesday morning Jerry is waiting for me when I come up the walk. His hair is parted a little crooked, but it is all combed with Vitalis. I check whether his heart has washed off. It is there and I'm still thinking about whether he took a bath last night and re-did the heart, or whether he did not take a bath at all, just put on a clean shirt, when he speaks to me.

"Meet me again today by the water founting," Jerry says as we pass into the front hall where Mr. Jenkins the principal is standing in a brown suit with his arms folded.

"Shhh!" I say.

Jerry glances back at Mr. Jenkins. "To hell with him," Jerry says, but quietly and right in my ear.

Maydean writes me a note during lunch count: DO YOU LOVE JERRY? YES____ NO____.

Before I can answer back, the teacher starts the six-weeks spelling review. I put Maydean's note in my desk.

Before recess, I check my socks, that the backs of them have not worked down inside my shoes. Jerry is waiting for me and we walk out to the bleachers again.

"Yep, Friday," Jerry says when we're settled. He's looking at his heart. He digs in his pants pocket and offers me a stick of Juicy Fruit. I say thanks and unwrap it slowly, thinking about what I might make out of the foil. Jerry takes two pieces for himself, unwraps them, rolls them together, says "Watch," and throws them in his mouth like popcorn.

We stare out at Rosemary and John's teams, who are playing for real today. Once, I forget and clap and scream "Yea!" when Sharon hits the ball into right field.

She throws down the bat and runs to first base. "She's deader 'n a doornail," Jerry says. "Shit! Ten to one, they've got 'er."

I'm thinking whether Jerry should have said that to me when he scoots a little closer. I have my hand on the seat, with my skirt

3

spread over it, and now he runs in his hand and gets hold of mine. His hand feels real warm and rough and a little wet. The wet part surprises me. I look back toward the building, checking if Miss Schumaker might be looking at us out the window.

Now we sit really looking at the ball game. Jerry is concentrating, you might say. But I am trying to memorize everything about Jerry's hand to check out with Maydean later. Am I holding it too tight or too loose? Suddenly, Jerry doubles back his middle finger and starts rubbing it slowly inside my hand.

I look at Jerry. He is looking extra hard at the ball field, his eyes kind of scrunched. I think he must have seen something awful and I look. Nobody is even up to bat.

On Wednesday it rains in the morning so we stay inside. When that happens, the girls play jacks in the corners of the room and the boys play rubber horseshoes in the hall.

Jerry waits for me after school and we ride on our bikes side by side until Bluebonnet Grocery, where he fishes in his pocket for two dimes, tells me to stay with the bicycles, goes in, comes out with two Grapettes. We drink them there under the dripping trees. I try not to get any around my mouth. Jerry fits his lips inside the bottle on purpose.

So his whole mouth is purple. "Want a kiss?" he asks and smacks me before I can decide for myself.

J-e-e-rry!" I say, like I know I'm supposed to, and turn away. He laughs and carries the bottles back in.

When I get home, Mother asks me why I'm late. "I had to go back and get my speller." I am careful not to open my mouth too wide. I race through the house to the bathroom. Anyway, the speller is partly the truth.

Thursday when Jerry goes to the board to diagram the sentence Miss Schumaker has assigned him, he drops another note in my lap. When Miss Schumaker gets all mad because Jerry has put an adjective on the subject line, I open the note in my lap. It has "I love Nelda" written a billion times on it, from one corner sideways, over and over, to the bottom. At the end it says, "If I decide they rite your

4

name on my arm, you get one of these ever day after that, FOR-EVER."

I re-fold the note and put it in my desk. I take off my glasses and fold them. I cross my arms and lay my head on them. It seems like all I am doing is folding things. I am too tired. I roll my head and pick out Jerry at the board.

He is all fuzzy around the edges but I can still see that some of his hair has gotten loose and is sticking straight up in back. I begin to think how my mother calls a cowlick a turkey tail, and which name is right.

Jerry is erasing his sentence after Miss Schumaker has told him to start over and do it right this time. He's not erasing neatly. He's doing it like swipe! swipe! making puffs of chalk. I squint and try to see the heart on his arm, but I can't. I don't know if it's because he's moving his arm too fast or because I don't have on my glasses.

I raise up and reach inside my desk. I feel Maydean's note and bring it out. I press it out on my desk and uncap my pen. I check NO.

The Noise Expert

I told my house mother that first day I'm not wearing my sweater to work at the airport. I didn't tell her that a sweater does not make a noise worth a flip. I only said, I'm wearing my nylon jacket or nothing. (It goes Shee! Shee! under my arms.)

That was just the beginning of the trouble I had here at Eats-on-the-Run, before I got things fixed about me and loud. Some people never will understand, but no matter. As long as Lonny and Imogene do. How I can't see my hands and feet without loud. How when it's quiet around me I start to fade like paints gone watery, soaking into the paper. How noise is like medicine and mother and daddy to me.

The only one who halfway knew in the beginning was Imogene. Her face is so shiny it looks on fire. First day, I said to her, "Please, Imogene, I don't like soft tacos. Just the ones that go Crack! I want four."

"Richy boy, you a sassy thing," Imogene said. "I gonna make you tacos when you bite 'em they 'splodes like hand gernades."

And every morning after that, when I opened the kitchen door, Imogene called out, "Here come Mr. Clatterty-bang!"

She was close. But it seemed like almost everybody else didn't care if I lived or died. "DBQ at DFW." Death By Quiet at the Dallas-Ft. Worth Airport. If I ever make a movie, that's what I'll call it. (I say DFW fast so people think I'm a pilot.)

It all started when they changed over from real to fake dishes. My

7

first job here at Eats-on-the-Run was supervisor of washing real dishes and silverware. I drew those plates off the line—slop to the right, paper to the left—then Crash! like two police cars on television down into the pre-rinse.

Imogene would kind of compliment me on it. She'd say, "Richy, you bustin' them suds like a giant o' sorts." Then I would hold my breath and make my chest hard.

I loved it best when a lot of dishes came through at once. They made more noise together. I knew people could see me. I knew I was standing there. My hands and feet showed up just fine.

And mornings, because of more cups and saucers. The cups sounded Puck! like they swallowed their own selves when they hit the water.

After the pre-rinse, I got to load the dishes in the dishwasher. Clunk! and Phum! It was great.

Silverware? Wires, bells, slinky toys. When I dumped the soak bucket in the sink, everybody in the kitchen looked around. Once the dishwasher was full, I was to tell Imogene and she'd come turn it on for me. The water started up with a roar and that's when I'd lean against the machine and re-tie my shoes. When I could feel the noise, I was Okay Operational.

Then came the day everything changed and I had to work hard to keep myself from disappearing.

I went in that day as usual and I washed dishes until after Flight 117 came through. (Those passengers are all hungry by the time they get to us. Eats-on-the-Run is not like your ordinary café—we got our busy times according to the airplanes on our concourse—we're special.)

By then it was afternoon and Mr. Perkins, my super who is not even as old as I am but who talked to the people at the Home about me working here, came in and said, "Richy, guess what? This is your last load of dishes."

I dried my hands quick on my apron and put them in my pockets. After I'd done a load, I'd keep my hands in my pockets as long as they'd let me because my fingers looked like soft pickles. They scared me 'til they got hard again.

I started to cry, thinking they weren't going to let me work at Eats anymore. Mr. Perkins said, "Wait, Richy! All I meant was, we're going to plastic."

If I had of known how hard it was to make noise with plastic, I would have kept on crying.

Now they put me out front cleaning tables and stuff. The first few days I missed the sounds of the dishes so much I thought about quitting, but what would I say: "I'm quitting because no one can see me anymore"? I whistled a little bit, but no one paid much attention to me. I had to think up new ways to make loud.

This is what I figured out: When I went to clean off a table, I folded the styrene soup bowl in half and crammed it in the small styrofoam coffee cup, then twisted it—so I got a Screech! Then poked that upside down into the jumbo styrofoam. If I caught the two cups just right, they sounded Pow! like boxers.

Next I took the plastic silverware (boy, is that name a laugh!) and folded it in a napkin and broke it. At first I just popped it with my bare hands but the plastic cut me up and Mr. Perkins said if I thought I should break it, be sure to roll it in a napkin first.

When I got through clearing the table, I was supposed to check the booth seats too. Then's when I found a new noise. If I saw a crumb or anything at all, I let fly with my rag, just hit that seat over and over until the thing bounced off. It felt good to be giving something a spanking. The vinyl was better than a behind for hitting.

Sometimes, especially if it was on the long seat by the divider, I'd pop the rag right next to a lady and she'd jump a mile. I guess she thought I was coming at her with that rag. "It's okay, lady," I'd say. "I have to clean the seats." This way I got to say something to the customers.

And every now and then through the day I managed a bunch of noise with the garbage sacks for the pitch-in. The sacks are folded up in a tight square, so I shook them out—four, five, six times if Mr. Perkins wasn't around—before I put my arms inside and took the corners clean to the bottom of the tub. It got to where everybody in the whole place would be looking at me when I finished.

So, between me screeching the styrofoam, popping the seat with my rag, and shaking the pitch-in sack, I was hanging on. I adapted, as my counselor at the Home says to do. And besides, I still got to wash the pots and pans in the afternoon.

That is until Lonny came from another Home, and Mr. Perkins said for him to take over my job of washing up the pots and pans. I hated Lonny right off. They should let you keep your first noises.

I don't care if I *did* get good with the fake dishes, I still loved my pots and pans. There was this one lid that sounded like a cymbal from Lawrence Welk if I hit it with a spoon just right. I always asked Imogene, "Did you use my lid today? I need to fix my head with it."

"Richy, you crazy!" she'd say. I liked her. She treated me great. I never heard her tell Lonny he was crazy or anything like that.

So I was really mad at Lonny in the beginning. I didn't say a word to him, not even hello when he came in, mornings. He'd say, "Hi, Richy," but I pretended I didn't hear.

Then we all found out Lonny couldn't remember anything. Sometimes he left his rag on the table. Or his spray bottle right in the middle of a table along with the ketchup and napkins. And his van driver had to come in and get him in the afternoons because he couldn't remember when to stop work.

After about a week, there Lonny is, standing beside me at the window one morning when I am on my break watching Flight 37 take off. Lonny's head is long and his chest is kind of caved in. He looks soft all over.

We are both standing there looking out, pretending we don't see the other one. I always keep my hands on the glass; I like to feel the rattle when a plane takes off. So when a 747 in the next gate turned around and started taxiing out to the runway, Lonny says, "You like noise, don't you?" Just like that.

I keep looking out the window and try not to grin. "How'd you know?"

"I been watching you," Lonny says.

We walked back together, but I told myself he came along with me because he didn't know when he was supposed to go back. From then on, when it was time for my break, I went back to the kitchen and told everybody, "I'm going on my break now. I'll be over at Gate 6."

"Okay, honey, " Imogene would say. "We come find you if we get a rush on."

And after I'd walk over there and be studying the runways real hard, I'd feel a person beside me and it would be Lonny.

I guess we looked funny, standing there in our white aprons and hats, both of us with our hands flat up against the glass waiting for Flight 37 to take off for London.

Finally one day Lonny said, "That airplane sound scares me to death."

I looked at him. He was staring straight out at the planes. "Then why do you come to the noise?" I asked him.

"Because I'd rather be with you and your noises than by myself," he said.

After that, I began helping Lonny remember more. Before, Mr. Perkins had had to tell Lonny a bunch of times about leaving his wipe-up rag on a table. Lonny would be back in the kitchen asking for another rag and Mr. Perkins would say, "Go look for your rag, Lonny. I bet it's on a table." Sometimes Lonny's eyes got red around the rims.

Now I would watch and when Lonny started to leave his rag on the table, I would bust out singing a Kenny Rogers song. It wasn't very long until Lonny caught on.

But pretty soon my own troubles started up again. One of our customers with a fur coat complained about me. Here's how it happened.

When I see something soft, I have to make more noise than ever. Otherwise, the soft will suck up my ordinary sounds and there I'll go, getting dimmer and dimmer.

So when this lady came in on an afternoon flight and threw her coat on the long vinyl seat, I made my way over there as soon as I could and started beating the seat beside it with my rag.

11

She already had a cigarette and coffee and was talking to her daughter. The first hit, she jumped sky high.

"Jesus! What is wrong with you?" she said, real loud, and the loud in her voice was nice but the words weren't. Her hair was pricked up like Woody Woodpecker's in front.

Most people jump and look at me if I beat the seat close to them, but they don't say anything. This time I didn't know what to say back. "I like the loud, is all."

"What kind of an answer is that?" she asked her daughter. Then she got right up and went to Mr. Perkins and said I had tried to hit her with my rag. She was traveling from one hospital to another with a nervous disorder, and I was the straw that broke the camel's back. Besides all that, she had a friend who knew a person on the airport board.

Mr. Perkins told her he was real sorry and he'd take care of it. He called me to go help Lonny with the pots and pans. At quitting time Mr. Perkins told me to wait to clean the long side seat until there was nobody sitting on it. That's all.

So the next day, I missed the Pop! Pop! of the seat because there was somebody on it practically all day. A kid ate a croissant all over it and Mr. Perkins sent Lonny to wipe up the crumbs. Lonny didn't even forget his rag. It all made my stomach hurt.

The next morning Mr. Perkins gave Lonny my job of changing the plastic garbage sacks. Lonny couldn't make a sound worth a dime with them. You got to hold on to the top tight and punch your hands up and out in front of you until the sack comes down like a parachute. I showed Lonny, but he only did little jerks down the front of himself until the sack opened. He was too soft.

The next day Mr. Perkins brought a pink plastic tub to my cart and told me not to break the forks and spoons, not even rolled in a napkin—just put them all together in a heap. And to stack in separate stacks the soup bowls, the cheesecake saucers, the divided plates. To put the small, medium, large drink cups all by themselves. He had caught on to me.

The day after that I couldn't get out of bed. I told my house father I had a sore throat. I lay in bed all that day, and the next and the next. The medicine they gave me made me feel funny.

The fourth morning my house father came in. "Richy," he says, "I talked to Mr. Perkins yesterday. I think your sore throat is better."

"Nobody cares about me anymore," I say. "I might as well not be there, what with Mr. Perkin's new rules."

"Go to work today, Richy," my house father says. "You remember what adapting means, don't you?"

Lonny was waiting for me at the service entrance. "Hi, Richy," he said. I didn't look at him. I went on in. I rattled my jacket hanging it up and got my apron and hat. Lonny was right there beside me.

"We fixed it," he said.

"Fixed what?" I said.

"Fixed your loud," he said. He took a little radio out of his pocket.

Imogene turned down her grill and came over. She reached for her purse on the shelf and brought out a package. It was wrapped in plastic and she handed it to Lonny but he was too soft to open it. I took it from him and broke out the hard plastic window with a good Snap! It was headphones and Lonny took them and plugged them in to the radio. Then he put the headphones on me and handed me the radio.

The music went straight to the middle of my brains. Drums up behind my nose. Guitars taking off on my tongue.

Imogene wiped her face on her apron and started grinning. I could see her lips moving. "Imogene to Richy . . . over!"

"I read you, Imogene." I must have said it real loud. Everyone in the kitchen looked around. Lonny had put a piece of tape over the volume button so it wouldn't go soft.

"Can you see me?" I asked them.

"Yes, but you've got to keep your radio on," Lonny said.

"And eat a lot of them loud tacos," Imogene said.

Then we all went back to work.

An Adventure Is Made For Having

From the time the boy had told her the plan, the girl daydreamed about the last day of her visit. The other four days she and the boy had played Monopoly and Slap Jack, teased the dog, and spied on their older sisters as the girls were doing dumb things like mooning over pictures of James Dean or bleaching the front of their hair with lemon juice.

This morning, while it was still dark, the boy had come into the guest room and jiggled her foot to waken her. She had already penciled the stuff into her diary: *Gainesville, Texas / June 25, 1950* —so she could start right in recording the adventure after it happened.

He called the thing they were going to do "bagging frogs,"and promised her it would be fun. His mother would fry the frog legs, and eating their catch for lunch would be the high point of the visit. In the late afternoon, the boy's mother was to drive the girl and her sister to Dallas where their parents would meet them for the rest of the trip home.

Of course, the boy wasn't about to let the girl touch his BB gun. She knew that. It would be her job to stand a little way out in the water while he shot at the surfacing frog, keep her eye trained on exactly where the widening ripple started, wade out to that point, and bring back the dead frog. In other words, she would be his hunting dog.

Anyway, it *was* his gun and it *was* his dad's cattle tank, and the

15

girl and her older sister *were* the visitors. That was one reason to keep the diary, to remember all the places they had lived. They sometimes got to go back to re-visit like this. Their father was in the military. He had brought them for only a little while to Camp Howze, but it was long enough for the girl's sister to make a friend at school.

The boy had promised that she would like the frog legs, that they tasted exactly like chicken, the way his mother fixed them—maybe better. All in all, it would be something to write about that first day back at school when the teacher assigned the theme about summer to be written while the textbooks were being issued. She would not title it "My Summer Vacation." Hers would be "My Summer Hunting Wild Game."

"But what about the cow stuff?" she asked, following the beam of his flashlight as they walked through the dry summer grass.

His uncombed hair stirred in the dawn breeze. "There's not any out in the water and you ought to be smart enough to step around what's at the water's edge."

They crossed over a little knoll and descended to the tank. There was a faint wafting of cool air off the water, but that didn't mean a thing. By eleven o'clock it would be a hundred degrees. This was Texas in the last week of June.

She bent to roll up her blue jeans, carefully folding them over and over so they would fit above her knees. "What do you mean, 'There's not any out in the water'?"

She had seen the cow plops all around the edge of the pond and it didn't make sense cows were smart enough to cut it out when they waded in to cool themselves in the parched summer afternoons.

"I told you, there's not any out where you're going," he said, fiddling importantly with his rifle.

"How do you know?" she persisted.

He looked at her. Maybe he was sick of her. Still, he had been pretty nice to her all week even though he hadn't known that she was coming. Their teenage sisters had planned the visit and at the last minute, the younger girl was sent along to be the boy's companion so he wouldn't spend the whole week pestering the older girls.

The girl was eleven and the boy was barely ten, but that was okay. She would forget that he was younger, if he was the means to an adventure. Nancy Drew had adventures. Clara Barton did. It was time she was having them too, but it seemed a little hard to find one. So she had said to herself, Put up with this stinking boy long enough to have an adventure.

The boy sighed, sounding grieved, but patient. "Cows have got more sense than to poop where they're fixing to drink, and if you don't hurry, it's gonna' be too late." After the sun rose and the day swooned hot, frogs were not as active. In the pre-dawn lull they cruised the pond, snapping at insects.

The girl stepped gingerly into the water that barely moved at the shoreline. Her toes disappeared in green ooze. She bit her lip and took another step, balancing with outstretched arms.

"What if the cattle come?" she asked.

"Shhhhhhhh! You'll scare the frogs." His voice was louder than hers.

"I don't care—you answer me!" She had some rights.

"They won't," he said.

"Yes, but what if they happen—"

"I'll take care of you, sissy," he said.

They settled in to wait for the dome of a frog's head to break the stillness. The dark water circled her white legs higher and higher as her feet sank in the mire. He cocked his rifle and studied the surface of the pond.

In a moment they were rewarded. A beginning ripple revealed two eyes about twenty feet beyond the girl. The boy fired, cocked the gun, fired again. There was a flurry, a plash, and the ripple deepened and hurried out in all directions.

"I got it!" he called. "I know I did. Go pick it up now."

She extricated one foot, then the other, and moved out. Each step was soft, with no promise of a firm bottom. Each foot twisted a quarter-turn before she could straighten it. She discovered her arms flailing the air to keep her balance and quickly put her hands on her

17

hips. Maybe the boy hadn't noticed. She concentrated on the exact center of the widening ripples. It was hard to keep looking there and watch her step too.

"Hurry up!" he called. "Get on over there. I've done it a billion times."

"Shut up!" she answered. "I'm going as fast as I can."

Arriving at the site, she gingerly reached down and began to grope, half fearing she would touch the frog. The slime filled her fingernails. Soon she felt a kick, and, closing her eyes, she grabbed. A large grayish bullfrog with a hole in its side mustered a few kicks as she raised it dripping from the water. She felt dizzy and desperate. "Can't you come get him?" she called. She had done her part.

The boy was reloading, though he still had plenty of BB's in the gun. "Hell, no. I've got my boots on. Bring it on in." He continued busily with his gun. "For crying out loud." She waded toward the shore. The frog gave one last furious twist. She tightened her grip, feeling it splutter against her face. Then it went slack.

The boy held open his game pouch. "Drop it in there." She did and leaned down to rinse her hands in the muddy swirl.

Now the boy shot repeatedly, shooting at anything, it seemed to the girl. She could have sworn he shot at dragonflies touching down on the pond. She waded out dutifully each time and groped for the frog. When she failed to find it, he told her she hadn't been fast enough. Once he said, "Hurry up and get the damned thing. Don't be a slow poke."

"Come out here and get it yourself, smarty-pants," she said.

"That's your job," he said, and spat boldly.

She was glad to be going home. He had gone braggy and ugly all of a sudden.

They had four frogs when the sun gilded the knoll and they heard the yard bell. It was strange, because his mother had not called them for breakfast all week. They got their own cereal and milk whenever they wandered into the kitchen.

"What does *she* want?" the boy asked.

"Yeah," the girl joined, trying not to sound too disrespectful.

Despite her care, the cuffs of the girl's jeans were crusted with mud and her blouse sleeves were wet. Her toenails were islands of silt and each fingernail harbored a half-moon of mud. She brushed back a strand of hair, at the same time streaking her face.

She had done it. She had had an adventure. She had rolled up her pants legs and gone straight into the tank and retrieved frogs. She had waded out past the cow manure, and with the prospects that dangerous cows and bulls might come.

"From the depths"—that's how she would put it when she wrote about it in the essay. "Battling unknown dangers." She would use "suddenly" several times. She would write "very dirty" to describe the edge of the tank and underline it—hoping the teacher would understand and nod approvingly at the way she had avoided saying "cow poop."

Of course, the end of the adventure was yet to come—eating the frog legs. She would be sure to tell about this in her essay. She would not tell her parents about any of the adventure, because her mother would say it was a wonder she had not drowned or been gored by a bull, and her father would say whoever heard of a girl doing such things. And when she came back the next summer, she would ask the boy to let her shoot the gun.

They started toward the house—he, limping in fake heroism with the weight of the frog bag; she, picking at the caked mud on her forearms.

The boy's mother was at the back door. "You children need to hose off before you come in the house," she said. The mother was pretty, kind of la-di-da and fancy.

"We got four frogs," the girl said.

"That's nice," the mother said.

"Remember you said you'd cook the legs for lunch?" The boy was wiping his boots furiously on the backyard grass.

"Oh Buddy," his mother said, "I don't think so now. There's been a change in plans. We're going to take the girls to Dallas right away."

The children's shoulders slumped. "Awwwww."

"Something's come up," the mother went on. "We've just

heard President Truman on the radio. There's a bad disturbance in Korea. The girls' parents called. Their dad may have to go on active duty. They're coming right away to Dallas to meet us."

"Active duty?" the boy said. "Gosh." The girl dribbled the cold water from the hose over her greenish legs. Gradually they turned white again. She rinsed her arms and slung them dry.

She would go in the house now. She would take off these things and put them in a plastic bag the boy's mother would provide. She would put on her clean blouse and skirt and they would go to Dallas, she and the boy being careful not to touch as they sat in the back seat with one of the sisters. And the frogs would lie, dead and stinking, in the corner of the yard all day, or until the dogs found them.

She walked slowly toward the back door in the early morning light. The title of her essay would be "War Ended My Summer Adventure." It reminded her of the "Heidi" film at school that had made her cry. She could still tell everything that had happened so far in the adventure. The thing was, she would never know how many more frogs they might have bagged before the sun got hot, and, if the frog legs really tasted like chicken.

Even though it was getting warm, she shivered in her damp clothes. She wondered if there might be other events, things she didn't know about right now, things to spoil the adventures she just knew were out there waiting for her.

Brush Boy

What are we dreaming of when we set out to live the life of a child? I lived my young days mindful and didn't know it. I know now I lived a life of edges, of standing with my toes curled over the side of a known world. It wasn't a theme—the lives of young frontier boys don't have themes—but it has stood me in good stead when I have been to the precipices of my life.

I was on the border from the beginning, for I was born in a small South Texas town on *la frontera*. Actually, they had moved the frontier back, in retreat, twenty years earlier. Too many damned *banditos* and too many floods, said the county *honchos*, of the original town located right on the Rio Grande, and so by night, they moved the county's records to a section of brushland a few miles north.

When the people who worked at the courthouse wakened the next morning, they had to hitch up their buggies and migrate through the chaparral to the re-established place of law and order. That's how my grandparents—he worked in the courthouse—came to live at the corner of 8th and Mahl in the small put-together town. One block east was my grandmother's aunt, and then another block away lived my grandmother's brother, who also worked in the courthouse. Down to the south, her sister had a quarter of a block— her husband was the tax collector—and so on. They all wanted to be near the courthouse and so they bought lots in this little town that sought to delineate the line between a new Texas county and the wildness of northern Mexico.

Another edge for me was the location of our house. My father, who also worked at the courthouse, established us on the southwest periphery of the town. One side of our dirt street had houses, but the other side was the beginning of heavy brush, a tangle of mesquite, *huisache*, sage and cactus with an occasional clearing where wild things came to drink at rain ponds. Sometimes the men went into this world and emerged with javelina and deer, or, without such luck, rabbit and rattlesnake. Everything south of our street was exotic, spooky, uncharted—thus, our playground of choice.

When I think of that tumble of undergrowth, and how I felt perfectly free in it, I connect it with my mother, who as freely let me go into that thicket, as she guarded me against the wilds of a bilingual world, which she viewed as a polyglot morass.

Sure, you could be hurt, running all over town and out in the brush. That was your business; it was a chance you took. On the other hand, running the gauntlet with words, being shoddy and dumb in the world of language, now that would certainly condemn you to a life of failure.

Very early on, I was turned loose. My mother would let me wander and do almost anything as long as I returned sometime. Looking back, I don't know if letting me roam was her conscious decision. Maybe it was just part of her fabric. She was a fighter, the first child in the family to go to college, the only Mexican at the college in San Marcos, and a young woman at that. She was always striving. She didn't want to be anything second best, and she didn't want to be a part of that possibility in her children either. Maybe this is where she got the notion that she should let me go unbounded.

But like many freethinkers, she chose her area of rigidity and that was language. I was not allowed to speak any English until I went to kindergarten, her theory being that I should learn Spanish completely before my mind was cluttered with another language. So I never spoke a word of English until I entered kindergarten, which was a strange enrollment in itself.

We happened to live on the side of town with the Anglo school and it was a special privilege for me, counted as a Hispanic though one grandfather's surname was Schunior, to go to their kinder-garten. The Mexican school on the other side of town did not have a kindergarten. This atypical arrangement was par for my family, mingled as we were for six generations north of the river. (When my mother went to college, everyone was baffled that she was Hispanic though with a surname of Schunior. She was instantly dubbed "Schuniorita.")

Still, I was the only one who did not speak any English that first day at kinder. I think I learned it quickly, but calling by different names the things I had learned in my heart another way—this sore-ness lingers in my dreams.

In my freedom to wander, I never could figure out my mother's mind on when I was late and when I wasn't. Would she be angry when I came in, or would she not say anything? What was *late*? She never defined it, and it would have been unheard of for a child like me to have a watch.

I tried to be back on time, whenever it was convenient. But if it seemed I was late, by the way the sun was, and I was having a great time, I told myself this was probably a day when she wouldn't think I was late.

When I wasn't exploring the edge of the world across the street with my friends Homero and Nestor, I wandered the streets among the houses of my vast "extended" family. They were always needing something, and a small, what-me-worry barefoot relative with his shirt buttoned wrong was their ready courier. For my part, I was totally attentive to whatever would occupy me this instant, that instant. It was a wonderful world.

I'd show up at the back door of my grandmother's house and she and her aunt would be preparing the noonday *comida*. She might give me a tortilla from the griddle and, waiting until I had quickly rolled it and bitten the end off, say, "Alfonso, do something for me." I almost always guessed right, what she wanted. "Go to your *padrino* and get our medicine."

It seems my grandparents got out of medicine often and I wondered, since they looked okay, what was perpetually wrong with

23

them.

Then they'd hand me a sack containing an empty brown glass cough syrup container. *¡Bueno!* and I'd push out the back door, stuffing the rest of the tortilla in my mouth.

When I got to Padrino Alfredo's house, he'd salute me, *¡Que hubo, Poncho!* and then, when he saw the sack, snatch it from me. "*Ay que—!* Give me that thing!" and disappear. He'd reappear and hand it to me roughly. It was plainly heavier now. "Tell them to quit bothering me!"

Even though I was young, I knew a few things about family relations. I never told my grandparents that Padrino Alfredo requested them to quit bothering him.

It was many years before I realized I should have been in the Guinness book, as the first and youngest drug runner in South Texas, handling, as I did, all the *mezcal* deliveries for *mi familia*.

They drank it neat, as an appetizer for the noonday meal.

That was only one of the ways my small life was lived on an invisible rim. I came to know the physical limits, the brinks of bodily disaster, but my mother gave me the great honor of learning them my way. I didn't know all this then, nor can I ever understand it completely. I did come to understand that my mother was different when the other kids told me what their mothers would say. Later on, during the war, my comrades would read letters from home and their mothers were still admonishing their little boys to be safe, be careful, watch out.

I remember climbing this chinaberry tree, stepping over on the steep roof of our house, going to the very top height and then walking that whole peak, straddling it, one foot on one side and one on the other. That conquered, I'd turn around and walk back to my starting point.

And I would climb up on the roof of the garage. Below, there were some plants—I forget the name of them even in Spanish—but they had large soft fronds with big flowers growing out of them, great for jumping in. I would conduct experiments, taking an umbrella and jumping down to this soft landing. Of course, the umbrella usually collapsed. My mother never, ever said a word of caution to me.

When I wasn't delivering mezcal, or walking on and jumping off rooftops, I might go across the street from the known world and do some exploring. On one of these occasions, I learned there were limits to my mother's will for my freedom.

It was a lazy summer afternoon and I and my friends, Nestor and Homero—by now my schoolmates as well, wandered across the road, out into the wilderness, just to ding around throwing rocks in an old pond, hiding in the undergrowth, jumping out to scare the others— the things boys did before there were soccer and *tae kwon do*.

All of a sudden, here was this herd of donkeys—wild *burros*. They had thick coats of hair and dark stripes on the shoulder. For sure, they were nobody's beasts of burden but absolutely wild. As I count them in my memory, there were at least forty. They were just out romping, kicking, playing around, like a circus come to town— really, the same as we boys were doing. I was purely astonished. I'd never seen anything like them.

I yearned to share the discovery. And the only one I knew to tell, who would listen to me, was my mother. So I ran home and into the house breathless. She was in the kitchen at the sink.

I banged in shouting, *Mamá! Mamá! No sabes lo que vi! Anda'amos—*

My mother turned quickly and wiped her hands on her apron. Her eyes flashed and she frowned. *Alphonso, se dice andábamos, no anda'amos.*

By this time I was jumping up and down. *Bueno, andábamos allá cerca del canal donde vimos munchos munchos burros!*

My mother put her hands on her hips. *No digas munchos—se dice muchos.*

Sí, Mamá, muchos burros que se revolvían en la tierra. It seemed terribly important to report their wild rolling in the dirt.

Alphonso, Alphonso. *Se revolcaban.*

What did it matter, if I said they mixed or they rolled in the dirt? At that moment my sweat began to sting all over. I had stayed in the kitchen longer than I wanted to. The kitchen was on the west and there was no breeze.

I was desperate. Maybe if I switched to English. "Well, anyway, there was all these hundreds of donkeys—"

Mamá winced. "Not there *was*...there *were!*"

Finally, I understood I could not give my mother these *burros* in any language. *Mamá* would not let me get past the words.

"Okay," I said, "I'm not ever going to tell you any more about *burros!*" and ran out of the house, slamming the door in a little fit of manly independence.

If that incident pushed me over the ledge of language, there was another donkey episode that brought me to a great divide, one of sure separation from my mother.

On another day, my friends and I were out in the brush again. Either we came upon them, or they came upon us. But we just couldn't get enough of this herd of *burros* so we hung around, bravely waving sticks at them, charging them to see if we could create a stampede. They were very little concerned.

After a while of grazing and drinking at the pond, a couple of *burros* began trying to mate, but the jackass was having a difficult time. It wasn't that the jenny was not being cooperative. Maybe they weren't on even ground. Maybe he was too ardent and thus, his aim inaccurate. Anyway, he wasn't achieving his goal.

We rested on our haunches and talked over their problem. After all, we'd seen dogs and livestock animals mating.

"He needs help," Homero said. Nestor and I agreed.

Homero was the oldest, and the tallest and toughest. "Get something to hold him with," he commanded and we scoured the edge of the clearing until we located an old piece of cardboard.

Not pausing to talk over the dangers of being kicked to death by wild *burros*, Homero rushed the beasts with his hand-held sex aid. Without any seeming notice or negative reaction whatsoever from the busy animals, and with Nestor and me cheering from the sidelines, Homero grasped the jackass's member and guided it home. Then the union was quite successful. Homero retreated and we three stood watching them, fascinated, marveling how our idea had literally taken hold. We could not have been more proud of ourselves. The brush scout troop's good deed of the day!

There were invisible borders, which if one crossed, one could never be repatriated. Implicit in the adventure was that we wouldn't be telling anyone how we had helped the *burros*. Ours was to be an anonymous charitable gift. Nestor said his mother would beat him silly if she knew what happened. Mine? I had already drawn the line. Donkey stories were *prohibido* with her. At this remove, I don't know if I inherently knew it was taboo to talk about sex with one's mother, or if I refused to talk *donkeys* at all with *my* mother.

The incident became a bond between us boys. Later, when we wanted to talk in code about how we had fumbled in the back seat of a car the night before with one of our girls, we'd say, "Remember *los burros!*" and burst out laughing.

So I existed in that marginal world, and the borders were my teachers. I would skirt the adult world of *mezcal* shots. I would learn how *Sí* could meet Yes on the rooftop of the world. I would come to understand how I could not cross the threshold of certain joys with my mother, like donkeys at play, be they *revolcando* or *flagrante delicto*, and how all these lines of demarcation, these fringes and margins early on taught me to step out in faith.

My First Near-Death Experience

You were too wonderful, Dutchie.

I have a hard time thinking of you now in an armchair some-where, your shirt tight around your belly, a pack of cigarettes peeking from your pocket, your calloused hands massaging the armrests as you make pronouncements to your wife about the news on television.

I want you to be eight, my lover for all time, with those huge white teeth, pinchy-winchy cheeks, that pale blond thick straight hair. When your mother cut your hair, she inverted a bowl over your head to get your bangs straight; thus your name.

Remember, I was in love with you in the third grade?

Down in the meadow where the green grass grows,
There sat Beverly pretty as a rose;
'Long came Dutchie, and kissed her on the nose:
How many kisses DID SHE GET?

Remember, how I told you that fact by chasing you at recess, pinning you down, spitting on you? You weren't too happy with the attention; still, I didn't know you were filing it away somewhere so you could provide me with my very first near-death experience.

It was convenient that we were neighbors. You lived at the bottom of my hill. We were connected by a long sloping alley filled with dagger-sharp chunks of gravel hauled in periodically to make the place passable. Most days we finished the walk home from school together, straggling the final couple of blocks as a twosome.

"Did you come with Dutchie today?" Mother would ask when I

slammed the back door.

"Yes, Ma'am." Whether it was true or not. She seemed to like the comfort of it.

But this near-death experience you gave me was in the summer. What I want to ask you, Dutchie, is, did you intend to? Was it *on purpose* or *just because*? In childhood, those were the two reasons for anything.

I thought we were just playing, like we'd always played, like we'd made up things to do to keep us from going crazy listening to the flies in the summertime in that small town. But did you remember me spitting on you, from way back during the school year? Did you tuck it away, and then do what you did that July afternoon to get even?

Or did you push me off, in love, like I spit on you at recess, in love?

Gray asphalt roof tile, and not much of a slope either. I went up the ladder first—no doubt because you dared me. If I took you up on the dare, you saw my panties. Probably why you dared me in the first place.

No doubt we had chicken dookey on our shoes already, you in those crazy hard Roy Rogers cowboy boots, me in my green strap sandals. We must have gone into the chicken yard specifically to climb onto that roof.

Now I see us sitting down, dangling our legs off the side, swinging them back and forth and looking down at the chickens, marveling at how small they are from our novel vantage. There are the Plymouth Rocks, Leghorns, Rhode Island Reds—I pronounce them "Rho Diland Reds."

We get into an argument, with you trying to make me pronounce the name right:

"Not 'Rho Diland Reds,' Stupid! Not 'Rho Di—'"

I mock you. "'Not Rho Di—'? Maybe 'Tho Pi—'?"

"No! Not that!"

"No! Not smat!"

"Stop it!"

"Chop it!"

Your face is scarlet. "Shut up!"

"Butt up!"

You jump up and stand behind me. You put your foot in the small of my back. You begin tapping harder and harder with the toe of your boot.

"Don't, Dutchie! Don't!"

But you continue and I grip the edge of the chicken house, leaning backward and holding on for dear life. You push harder and I'm flying out into space, not comprehending what has happened enough to be scared, just thinking, "Whee! So *this* is what it's like!"

The chickens proverbially acting startled and foolish as an eight-year-old featherless no-beaked chicken plops down in their midst, this creature so lacking in dainty, grain-picking, one-foot-down-and-then-the-other balance.

Did your mother pick me up and note my rolled-back eyes? No doubt. Did you, Dutchie, run in your tough little Roy Rogers boots to hide in the basement? I doubt it. You'd already told your mother I had *fallen* off. You stayed right there breathing Frito breath on me, seeing my panties all you wanted to. If I had wakened I would have given the standard reply, "I hope you get your eyes full, Dutchie!"

And that's how you taught me about eternity. When I woke up, Mother was carrying me up the hill, over the treacherous chunks of gravel.

They say that when I regained consciousness, I was moaning, saying things out of my head. I was washed, put to bed, my father called home from work. The doctor arrived and I had come *to* enough to be embarrassed when he pulled down the covers and put his stethoscope near one nipple. My scratches and bruises were treated with mercurochrome.

I lay in bed for three days—"keeping still," for the suspected concussion. But nobody explained, so I thought it was punishment for climbing up on the chicken house.

I had plenty of time to ruminate. If I saw Jesus or a beckoning figure, if I was in a tunnel moving toward the light, if I had a choice

31

of going or staying, these things I do not know many years later. What was the name of this black hole I had fallen into? I know that you, Dutchie, had taught me about the spirit world. I had been off somewhere, had taken the longest trip of my short lifetime.

For a while that afternoon, the world had existed, some way, without me. Preposterous! Magic! How could that be?

And then there was the golden treasure of regaining consciousness, asking, "What happened to me?" Waking up alive, the darkness harmlessly receding at the outer edges of my vision, my mother's face and comforting hands, the redemption of my own pillow, the white bed linens, the pale yellow light of summer suffusing the room. Years later I would remember how much I loved life that afternoon.

In the hours and days that followed, I was special to myself. I examined the scratches, felt the knot on my forehead, the bruised elbow. By thinking about it, I managed to foresee being an invalid the rest of my life. "Invalid," a word one said slowly, sadly, often used with "sick and afflicted," which had a nice chiming.

I ordered pears and crackers, confusing the food of choice for diarrhea with the food of accident. I managed to avoid chicken soup.

Dutchie, you came to my window one afternoon, scratching on the screen to get my attention.

"Psst! Psst!"

I pull the sheet tight across my pajamaed chest. "Go away! I hate your guts!"

You are undaunted. "You killed Biddie Sue."

"Biddie Sue?" I rise up suddenly. "I killed Biddie Sue?" A smile and goose bumps break out.

"It was my mother's favorite *Rhode Island Red*." This, you over-pronounce, determined to finish the fight.

I concede. For this is one of the proudest moments of my life. After eight years of existing, I have made a difference.

"I did? I did?" I forget all about hating you.

"Squashed her flat. We had to eat her that night for supper."

You keep standing there, Dutchie. "My mother said I had to come say I'm sorry." You pick up a rock and skip it down the alley.

"I'm sorry, hear?"

I rearrange the cover, thinking what to say. There must be prescience, hint of a lifetime ahead with a long string of guys saying, "I'm sorry, hear?"

You try again. "I'm not leaving until you say okay."

"It's not enough to say you're sorry." I fidget with the covers, get very busy making a tight band across my chest. Years later, I will recognize the moment: I have you by the *cajones*.

"Okay, *what* then?" You are ready for the *coup de grâce*.

There is a bit of proper shame left in me. I pull the sheet over my face. "You have to tell me you love me."

But when I turn back to the window, you are gone.

I resume my meditation. On trust, for one thing. How you could love somebody to pieces and think you wanted to marry them and vow to chase them at recess, and hope they would chase you, and maybe catch your sash and tear it from the waist of your dress so that the rest of the day your hand was surprised by your midriff's cool exposed flesh. . . .

Or how you could chase them and catch them and brand them with your spit tattoo—and still later, much later, they might just want to see what would happen if they scootched you closer and closer to the edge of a chicken house. . . .

It was the difference between getting love and getting attention.

On a less philosophical note, the experience had left me with a permanent aversion to barnyards. I would never look again with envy at those pictures in my books of rosy-cheeked servant maidens throwing seeds from their clean white aprons to colorful barnyard fowl. I knew what was on the bottom of the girls' shoes.

Years later, Dutchie, it scares the living daylights out of me to think of having the living daylights knocked out of me. A trial eternity for me while you scrambled down off the roof, ran in and told your mother, she phoning my mother, my mother drying her hands as she takes the steep back steps two at a time, forgetting the cake in the oven, hobbling down the rocky alley.

It wasn't much of any time before you got over being scared they were going to put you in jail and I got over hating you. But it was a while before I got to play with you again. I think we could only play at my house from then on. Something safe like a board game on the porch, I sitting cross-legged, my dress stretched over my knees, a little well poked down in the triangular cavity so that if your eyes got past the band of skirt stretched knee to knee, a second obstacle—the crumbled lap of my dress, would stop your curiosity cold.

I was guarding my sex. Still, I couldn't help yearning for you to say, just say you loved me. Love was all in the words. I was yet to discover that sex and love sometimes had a connection.

When did we fade from each other's side? After a while, we didn't walk home from school together. We didn't play together in the summer, on the porch or anywhere. Perhaps we got put in different classrooms at school. Assuredly at recess you began playing baseball and football with the boys and I joined the girls in cheerleading and baton twirling. No more games of chase, no more spit for love's sake.

It's just as well. You surely were not as gorgeous at twelve as at eight, although by then, of course, your face had grown to fit the size of your front teeth. My own comeliness? Ultimately I got a training bra. A training bra? God, I can't think *why* now.

In the tunnel of my memory, you grow smaller and smaller, lunging back only once, when your father died in a boating accident trying to save one of your friends. At the news that summer morning I sat on the back steps, tears dripping between my knees onto the concrete walk, aware for the first time that death could get *us*, the ones on this block, if not in the chicken yard, then on the local lake.

And then you moved off again, down the tunnel reserved for all the classmates who got lost from those that were fond of them, from those who stand about at parties and say loudly, "Whatever happened to old—?"

Let's meet back at the seesaws, Dutchie, find out how we turned out, share some memory of an age when the present was all there was. Are you moving toward the Light, Dutchie? The River Styx? Lethe? Jesus coming to cross you over Jordan?

Dutchie, if I found you today, maybe I'd run after you until I tackled you. I'd straddle you and. . . . I'd spit on you real good! Then, while I had you down, I'd thank you for kicking me off the chicken house, for the bravado of your little Roy Rogers boots, for the lessons your accidental malice taught me:

When you're high with a friend, do not tease;

That there's a darkness (if you're lucky, a trial darkness) beyond the *you* that is *you*—

That you can love somebody even after chicken shit comes between you—

That there's a difference between eschatology—death, judgment, the end of things, and scatology—the study of excrement.

In case you're waiting breathlessly, here's the word across the years: It's okay if you couldn't love me, Dutchie, or (as I like to believe) you couldn't tell me that you *really* did. It's enough that you taught me the difference between death and chicken shit. Death is permanent. Chicken shit washes off.

The Only Dancing Dog In Captivity

When Lauren closed her eyes, large Dalmatian spots danced behind her lids.

It all started with the characters Chesney refused to be in the second-grade Halloween play. Absolutely not a butterfly or a doll, Chesney reported to Lauren and David one night, licking sideways to get a piece of stray spaghetti.

"Why not? Those are the choices for the little girls, aren't they?" David countered.

"Oh, David." Chesney jiggled her fork. "No way. I would *hate* it." It had taken Lauren most of the year to get accustomed to a little girl calling her father by his first name. And hating so many things. But Chesney had come that way in the marriage package.

"So what did Mrs. Evans say when you told her?" Lauren asked.

"She said, 'Okay, but what will you be?'"

"And you said—?"

"I'll be the Only Dancing Dog in Captivity," Chesney said. "But the boys all screamed they wanted to be it."

David reached for another roll. "Then what did Mrs. Evans say?"

It occurred to Lauren that they were beginning to sound, in questioning this child, like the attorneys that they were.

Chesney smiled her victory smile, revealing a missing tooth. "She said, 'Certainly, Chesney. You'd make a good dog.'"

So now, as Lauren sat at the sewing machine resting her eyes, all she saw were dog dots. The Only Dancing Dog in Captivity was a Dalmatian and the costume had required three evenings so far.

"Chesney!" she called. "Come for a try-on."

"I'm busy."

"Come any-hoo!"

"Maybe later."

Lauren eliminated the singsong. "Right now, missy."

"Okay, okay," Chesney said, bursting from her room.

"You need to let me help you step into it," Lauren said. "Take off your jeans."

"I'll go in the bathroom," Chesney said. "I don't want you to see me."

"But you might get your foot hung on the zipper and break it."

"No I won't. I'll sit down to stick my legs in." And Chesney was off.

In a moment, Lauren heard Chesney chanting, "So! So! Suck your toe! All the way to Mex-ee-co!" It might be a while.

Chesney's mother had been killed on the freeway one afternoon four years ago on her way from work to pick up Chesney at daycare. David told Lauren that he had grieved so much at first he thought he would die also until he realized he had to live for Chesney.

He and Lauren had met at a law association party. He liked her for being tall and funny. He said she made him laugh that night for the first time in months. Lauren liked David's decisiveness, and his sandy hair and light eyes that reminded her of her dad.

When he told her about Chesney, she told him about her favorite niece, same age, back in her hometown. Later, when he asked her to marry him, she at first refused, pleading ignorance of mothering. "Why can't we just go on the way we are?"

"Because I'm old-fashioned," David had replied. "I want to be a family with my two favorite women."

So this was how she got to be sewing a dog costume for a Halloween play.

"You girls are silly not to buy the costume," David had said earlier in the week, meeting them on their way to the sewing shop as he came in from work. It was Lauren's week to leave her law firm early and pick up Chesney from school. "After all, it is spook season."

Before they married, she had admired David's clearly stated opinions about the way things were. But now his pronouncements about Chesney seemed arbitrary and over-simplified.

"But it's no ordinary Halloween costume," Lauren said, taking from her purse the picture Mrs. Evans had sent home. "With this play they're trying to get away from witches and axe murderers—you know, reduce the violence quotient." The drawing showed a spotted dog body, a skull cap with wired ears, matching mitten paws, and a long healthy tail.

All of that was to make Chesney look like a dog. A dancing dog required a red pleated neck ruff and conical hat with pompon.

"Whatever you want, Sweetie." David had shrugged and kissed her cheek. "But she'll work you, for all you're worth. Don't say I didn't tell you."

Lauren turned toward the car, where Chesney had already let herself in and buckled up. "It's not exactly what I want; it's what's important to her."

Actually Lauren would have preferred a seamstress out of a Dickens' novel, a humble woman in gray who would come to the house, measure Chesney, say motherly things to them both, and return the next day with a dancing dog costume.

In lieu of that, she would see if there was any residual skill in her from the sewing class her mother had insisted she take in high school. And Chesney would be filled with joy at the specialness of her dog suit.

For details were something David had not been able to give Chesney in her short life. David grabbed the first book handy on her shelf for her bedtime story: Chesney required the third chapter of *The Girl With the Toads*. He fastened her hair with a silver barrette he found in the top dresser drawer: she cried that it didn't match her gold belt buckle. He told her to use her brown crayon if she was out of black: she pushed her picture under the couch and left it there.

Lauren remembered her own particularized girlhood: the Amanda doll, the red patent shoes one Easter, her Mary Poppins book with its cover worn slick by her touch.

So she had shopped for tennies and minis with Chesney. She had learned to French-braid Chesney's hair. She had let Chesney squeeze stars and hearts out of the cookie press on Saturday afternoons.

The dog costume was terribly important to Chesney. And through it maybe Lauren would gain points with Chesney as someone with whom she must now share her father.

As Lauren sat waiting for the dancing dog to emerge from the bathroom, David clicked the front door lock and crossed the room to her. "How are you?" he asked, bending to kiss the top of her head.

"Tired."

He threw his briefcase on the couch. "You brought it on yourself," he said. "You and Chesney are overdoing it on this costume."

"Can't I say I'm tired?" she asked. "Is it wrong to be truthful—one lawyer to another?"

He ignored her. "If you have to do it, just sew it up any old way. It doesn't matter."

"It matters to Chesney," Lauren said.

He slouched in a chair. "I'm beginning to think she matters more to you than I do."

But later he seemed ashamed of himself. "No prob!" he said, when Chesney told him that she needed a circus wagon for the Renowned Clown to transport the Only Dancing Dog in Captivity onstage.

He went immediately to the alley and returned with a large box, calling over his shoulder as he disappeared into the garage, "Don't come out, either of you women. I want it to be a surprise." Lauren wondered if his command was a ploy to keep them from slowing him down with suggestions.

At eight David invited them to a showing. She had to admit it was cute. He had taken Chesney's wagon and taped the box to it. He'd cut a window on one side, with bars—to contain the ferocity of the Dog in Captivity—then sprayed one side of the box with a bit of leftover powder blue paint. She started around to inspect it. The final touch was big curlicues of glitter. He had worked nearly an hour.

"Oh, David!" Chesney said. "It's beautiful!"

David moved to Lauren's side. "See?" he murmured. "She's happy. Things don't have to be such a big deal."

Before Lauren could answer, Chesney shrieked. "It isn't finished!" She was standing on the far side of the wagon.

"C'mon, honey," David said, "it doesn't need to be fixed up except for one side. You're only going to ride across the stage in it. No one will see."

"We circle around." She began to cry. "We go back and forth."

"Are you sure?" David said. "Are you absolutely sure you go both ways on the stage?"

"I'm positive." Chesney wept full-fledged now.

David's face clouded. "It's your bedtime, young lady. You're all tired out. Come here and kiss Daddy good night."

She came reluctantly, fists smearing her tears.

He knelt down. "Go in with your mother," he said. "I'll see what I can do about the wagon."

Chesney drew back. "She isn't my mother!" she said. "She's Lauren."

Sometime after midnight, David came to bed. Lauren lay still, resisting the urge to ask him if he'd finished. He sighed heavily and mumbled to himself, "Damned particular women."

The night of the play, Chesney was too excited to eat her supper. David said helpfully, "Dogs always eat, and eat fast."

"I'll eat. Later." Chesney had figured out how to be borderline obedient.

The play opened with a number of grinning flowers on baby-fat stems. They lined up, swayed together in the musical breeze, and tiptoed away on cue at the piano's reprise.

Next came the butterflies flitting about on tissue-paper wings.

In the thickening plot, dolls appeared, cheeks rosy, arms akimbo, and then cowboys, twirling ropes, tugging at neckerchiefs.

Giraffes ambled onstage. A small bear on a leash lunged forth. And then a smiling clown walked out, pulling a powder-blue circus wagon. Lauren reached for David's hand. The wagon squeaked a little as the clown paraded it, circling the stage.

"She was right," David whispered. "It's not just a left-to-right thing."

The wagon stopped mid-stage. Emerging from the cage was—could it be?—"Yes!" Mrs. Evans announced from her microphone position, "The Only Dancing Dog in Captivity!"

Chesney extended a brown mittened paw from one end of the box, then the other paw, hauling herself carefully to the floor on all-fours. Her wire-strengthened tail, springing from captivity, wagged in friendly greeting.

The red pleated collar had slipped up over Chesney's mouth and she adjusted it with one paw. Then she checked her little pointed hat, sewn to the doggie headgear.

The clown pulled the wagon upstage and the music began. "How much is that doggy in the window?" Chesney smiled and the brown muzzle lines on her face crinkled.

She pranced. She cavorted. She pirouetted. She wagged her tail to the audience. When the song ended, she curtsied and climbed into her cage.

The act took at least a minute—maybe ten seconds more. But Chesney was glorious. Magnificent. Outstanding.

David leaned toward Lauren. "See there?" he said, as if suddenly trying to prove something to her. "I told you she'd be great."

When the program was over, they found Chesney in the hall, reliving her stage performance in dips and bows for a little friend who had only been a flower. As Lauren and David approached, they heard Chesney say to the other child, "We didn't buy it anywhere, Silly. My *mother* made it."

At this David slipped his arm around Lauren.

She whispered, "Did you hear that? And it only took fifteen hours of sewing."

He hugged her close. "Where's my reward? I spent three hours on the cage and I'm still just Daddy."

"Eighteen hours for the parents equal one minute on stage for the kid," Lauren said.

David laughed. "Must be the magic formula."

Lauren looked closely at David. She would never tell him a speck of blue glitter had made a round-trip commute that day on his nose.

Take Cover

Once, sitting in bed, I slit a new blanket as I tried to cut a piece of construction paper, fighting the torque of my mother's sewing scissors with my awkward left hand. Of course, the blanket's looks were ruined and my mother was angry. But the story I am telling now is of a different bed covering, a bedspread.

Sometimes the web of memory catches it as Snow White's picnic cloth. The chipper bluebirds take its corners in their animated beaks and hold it up as backdrop for a movie title. Other days, it is that hallowed cloth in the lore of religions let down from heaven or raised up to it, full of prayer objects or holy animals.

My grandmother would say it had character. True. The bedspread was unique, not inferior, to flesh-and-blood creations walking through other stories.

My mother's bed smelled of talcum powder. It was my father's bed too, but he was a lump on the other side, snoring quietly when I came in the pre-dawn, trying not to startle my mother as I touched her. "I had a bad dream," I would whine.

Mother never asked me what it was about, only "Well," and opened the covers to receive me. I knew to crawl in and turn away in the curve of her arm. "Make a spoon," she'd whisper. I fell asleep again immediately and slept safe until dawn.

Today, I acknowledge she was an adult, had done a mountain of work the day before, had an agenda the next day. Today, such a child as I would be counseled, scheduled for a sleep clinic, dosed with a drug at bedtime. Mother took me in, night after night.

45

Came the day a young woman of our acquaintance was put to bed in my parents' bed. Her illness, I was told, was ladies' troubles. Actually, she was about to miscarry.

I think Faitha must have been a young missionary, probably up from Central America on furlough. We were a way station for such. They would come for a week, the husband preaching on Sunday morning, the wife demure in the second pew. She would be allowed to speak that night, her talk introduced as a devotional, not a sermon. She would talk about the women and children, how children raised other children, how she combined Bible study and nutrition classes in their apartment living room, and, in the end, how God provided everything she and her husband needed for their stay on the mission field.

The words of the missionaries brought dread. They brought us the news that God was holding us personally responsible for saving the world from hell. These people were doing what we weren't.

There would be an invitation to go. "The fields are white unto harvest," the husband would shout when the choir paused between verses of "I'll Go Where You Want Me to Go, Dear Lord."

My father, as hosting minister, looked anxious and sad and expectant from his stance in front of the altar table. Once I asked my mother, If I surrendered to be a missionary, would Daddy be happy? She said that wasn't a good enough reason.

Anyway, I knew I couldn't surrender to be a missionary. What would I do if I had a bad dream in Africa?

It so happened I was home from school the day Faitha miscarried. I had had a stomach upset the night before. Mother believed a person should stay quiet for twenty-four hours afterward, so I had to content myself with playing bed games all day. But I begged until Mother let me go in and sit beside Faitha on the big bed; that is, if I promised not to snuggle in beside her but to remain on top of the bedspread.

Faitha was on my father's side of the bed, her legs supported by a pillow. She was a dainty thing, very pretty, I thought, with long reddish hair and wavy bangs. She seemed to be just lying or sitting there, not really sick; that made two of us who were perfectly all right with nothing to do. Faitha let me comb her hair.

The bedspread was a beautiful Belgian-made white cotton, one with candlewick texture and a heavy hand-tied border fringe. Only now do I have the words to describe it. Then, it just *was*, but even a young child knew it was too nice for the parsonage, that my folks could never have dreamed of buying it. The banker's wife, the richest lady in town, had picked it out and given it to us, probably in gratitude for some ministration of my father. It had a kind of sanctity.

When Mother made the bed with it, as she did on holidays or when we had company, the whole room looked like a department store display. The spread was so heavy and white, it graced everything around it like prayer or snow. I liked to dig my fingertips into the thick raised double diamonds and figure eights of the design and extract them slowly, allowing for an instant of delicious entrapment by the tight nubs.

On this day, this one day that holds in my memory like those tenacious hobnails of my mother's best spread, I excused myself from Faitha's sweet company for a moment and went into my father's study to take from his desk drawer a bottle of black India ink.

Maybe I had borrowed it before. Maybe I thought it, with its curious curved dropper shaped like a tiger's claw, was something I could not do without for the picture I was drawing. I am sure of two things: I wanted to impress Faitha, and I did not understand the permanency of India ink. I brought the ink bottle back to Faitha's bed and spilled three blobs the size of quarters on Mother's beautiful symbol of gentility.

Faitha had her eyes closed and I quickly lapped the spread over so the ink didn't show. Then a curious thing happened. When I went off to play somewhere else, Faitha apparently turned on her side and, getting a little of the spread tucked between her legs, bled profusely on it.

Later that day, Faitha called sadly from the bathroom for

Mother, a long time the two women in there, I standing in the dark hallway regressively sucking two fingers, listening to Faitha's crying, Mother's murmuring comfort.

At last they came out, Faitha trembling and crying, white and almost collapsing as Mother helped her walk. Years later, when Mother told me Faitha had miscarried the fetus into the toilet, I burst into tears. But what I thought of then was the bedspread.

For now, Mother restored Faitha to her bed and I carefully watched Mother's face as she pulled her prize, blood-soaked, from the bed. When she saw the India ink, her mouth opened wide, then closed, and she cast an angry glance toward me, for she knew immediately what had happened. But she checked herself and didn't speak, deferring at the moment to Faitha's anguish.

She soaked the spread in a washtub, first in cold water, then in a bleach mixture. Faitha's blood came out; my India ink did not. Not then and not ever.

So Mother put the spread away, folded on a closet shelf for years, still heavy and luxuriant, still stained, still too good for the rummage sale. I know she was grieved. The spread was one of the few objects she had ever been able to take pride in without the guilt of vanity.

When I married and hadn't enough bedding in a cold climate, she gave it to me. "Here," she said, in the only reference she ever made to my transgression, "it's got your signature." She smiled, a guarded teasing smile at the edge of memory.

Later, summer evenings, my kids lay on the spread in the backyard. They delighted to imprint their faces with the designs, trooping in to bath time bearing its pocky signature on their cheeks. They further delighted in the three firm black spots of India ink, a reminder that their very own mother had once been a foolish, careless child.

The bedspread fought on and on. Now in a second generation, it refused to wear out enough for *me* to give it away. Next it attended state university with a son. I have a vague vision of it draped over an old couch in a college-town makeshift apartment.

But I get ahead of myself. Some time in the life of the spread, I ripped the heavy, tied fringe from it and trimmed a poncho. It was a period in my life when things I loved were slipping away from me, and I was comforted by the constancy of the fringe on my long walks, drumming against my thighs in a steady rhythm, not letting the garment twist on me or billow out when the wind stiffened.

And then the poncho took on a life, or rather, wrapped itself around one. We were high in the mountains of Tamaulipas, observing a feast day in a village we had hiked to from the main road. (No, I was not there as a missionary. Was I still too afraid of my dreams?)

The poncho lay so well on my shoulders that I knew immediately when someone behind me fingered the edge. I turned and saw an old woman, a *viejita*, with a tangle of children around her. Seeing her shiver—maybe in fear, certainly in cold, I found it easy to slip the poncho over my head and hand it to her.

But that's only an edge of the story. The bedspread itself was, by this time, traveling toward a dual destiny.

Sometimes I remember it, after its college stint, in the back of our van on the way home from a picnic. We come upon a fresh accident. After my husband has pulled the man with the opened scalp from the window of his boiling overturned truck, we lay him on that spread and swaddle him in it against the onset of shock. When the ambulance comes, does the spread go to the hospital with him, or remain along the roadside? Nights, lying under a more modest coverlet, I can fill a blank in the dark, wondering which. Times like these I would go to my mother if I could, pretending the simple question was a nightmare.

Other times, I know without a doubt the bedspread was the covering that launched itself one night on the tide. We were camped on the seashore, thinking we were far enough up into the dunes. Our sleep was thick from a day of ocean air, and when the water stole in around our cot legs, we were a while waking. Only then did we discover a number of our camping items had moved out to sea, stolen by the moon.

In this memory, it is Faitha's and my bedspread, and Mother's— always hers of course—peaking with the waves, riding like a joyous surfer, sticking as close to the waves as the moonlight. It is out past the second sandbar, irretrievable, undulating like the bedding a simple good housewife might billow over and over when no one is around to watch. Just for the pleasure of seeing it float on air. Just to make the morning calm, after a night of tears and remorse, or sweat and love.

Regardless of its end, the memory wraps me in the white of mourning, grieving that the dreams of my mother could not be realized, remorseful that I canceled out such a simple one, pride in owning a fine thing.

And do the words of the story pronounce their own truth, say that, sometimes, ink is stronger than blood? Say how inked words on a page may carry the soul of a long-ago unborn child once more into the light, place it tenderly on a candlewick spread, gather a mother, her young daughter, a friend around it? How a story can be at once resurrection and absolution?

At One Stride Comes The Dark

Whenever Mavis tried to tell her mother how she was dedicating her life to bareback riding, her mother stopped what she was doing, put her hands on her hips, and looked straight at her. "Mavis, we are not white trash. I don't want to hear another word about the circus."

Urgency was barreling down on Mavis. She had chosen light pink and purple for her costume, and had several times managed to put her hair in a bun high on the back of her head, borrowing a little wreath of plastic flowers from her mother's tray to put around it. If she didn't start practicing right away, she might as well give up on the idea. Later, her legs might get spotted and jiggly, or she might forget how necessary it was to love the horses.

The captions under the circus pictures inthe *Locksville Leader* stressed that the performers were constantly practicing. That was why, the summer she was eight, Mavis brought up the subject of Dixie right after supper the first night. And to soften Root up, she asked him right *before* supper why his name was Root.

Mavis knew why her name was Mavis. Her mother had told her. "When I was carrying you, I was simply mad for that square red can of Mavis talcum powder." Mavis also knew that Root was short for Rupert, but she was willing to be dumb each time she asked.

As for Dixie, Root's black and white mare, Mavis would have to work up to the big question of riding her alone. Tonight she would ask Root to tell her Dixie's story again. Very soon, if he didn't offer to take her behind him, she would ask. Later, at just the right moment, she would ask to ride Dixie alone.

51

The other three summers that she had come to the Panhandle, Aunt Regina had insisted she ride behind Root. That had been okay; she would take any practice at all for her coming role in the Locksville Community Circus.

Her mother didn't think it was a good idea for the circus to be composed of hometown people. "Mr. Trewell should leave the funny business to Charlie Chaplin and stick to selling groceries," she said. About other mothers who sold cotton candy, she said, "They are making a spectacle of themselves."

Mavis had once ventured to say hello to Mrs. Lumpkins, who played the piano at church but also directed a trained dog act in one of the side rings. Mavis could swear, from personal experience, that Mrs. Lumpkins was not white trash, nor was she making a spectacle of herself.

They would let you be part-time, like Mrs. Lumpkins, but Mavis was planning to make the circus a vocation. If people could dedicate their lives to Jesus in the Baptist church, she could dedicate hers to the circus. When she got to high school, like Root was now, she would ask her mother if she could live at the livestock show grounds where the circus stayed. Her mother would probably like that.

If Mavis didn't get to do bareback riding, she would be a trapeze artist. During the winter, she worked out on her backyard trapeze, acknowledging the crowd when she balanced no-hands on the bar, or hung by one leg, or hung by her toes (though her hair got leaves in it when she did that). But this was only in case they had too many people in the bareback riding act. Horses were her first choice.

When Mavis asked about Root's name, he said, "Because I'm a big overgrown carrot."

"No, *really!*" Mavis begged.

"Short for rutabaga," Root said. He liked to squeak the swing idly as he waited for supper, dragging his heels, not going nearly as high as Mavis thought he should.

"You're kidding me." Mavis twirled in front of Root until her skirt billowed. He would play along with her.

"Is it 'cause you wear boots?" she asked, running up close to his fresh-washed face when he moved forward, inadvertently spitting on him a little in the throes of rhyming.

Root reached out and grabbed her—exactly what she wanted—and trapping her between his legs, dug his heels into the boards and lifted her high in a wide swoop of the swing. "Little city critter on a buckin' bronc!" he said. She screamed and held on to his hard thighs.

When Aunt Regina heard Mavis, she came to the screen, a bowl of peas in one hand grasped by a yellow hot pad. Aunt Regina was a tall strong woman who had never had a husband. Or a permanent or a manicure. Aunt Regina did not mind how often Mavis fingered the veins on the back of her hands or rippled the skin on her freckled arms. She had let Mavis teach her how to play Old Maids. Then she had taught Mavis dominoes. When they were too tired to play anymore, she let Mavis rest her head on her bosom when they sat in the swing together for a while before bedtime.

Aunt Regina and Root, her younger brother by twenty-five years, lived alone in the house, though the hands came in every day for lunch and supper, and some of the other six brothers and sisters were always driving out from town or flying in from across the country to stir the bills around on the roll-top desk in the den.

Mavis's mother was one of those, but she didn't like to come visit them at the homestead. She said it made her sad, thinking of Mavis' grandparents, Rupert Senior and Dora, who'd been gone since before Mavis was born. So when she brought Mavis in the summer to stay, she went away that same afternoon. Mavis tried to look sad when her mother left.

"Rupert Junior," Aunt Regina said, "put her down right now! You'll have her so worked up her dinner won't digest properly."

Root grinned and stopped abruptly, opening his legs, lifting her down with gawky young hands already wide and red from farm work. After Aunt Regina went on to deliver her peas to the long dining table, Mavis climbed into Root's lap and whispered, "I'm going to marry you, Root." He had such pretty white teeth, and a horse.

Root would never say no to her marriage proposal, just "You're already my niece, Miss Mavis-Davis."

The first summer, when Mavis was five, Aunt Regina invited her to come to the farm for two weeks, and Mavis heard her mother tell Aunt Regina in a whiny voice over the phone that she hoped Mavis wouldn't be an extra care. Mavis made a note to find out what an extra care was and not be it. She didn't want to do anything that would keep her mother from letting her be in the circus.

Mavis's mother hung up the phone and acted cheerier than she had in a while. She told Mavis that Mavis was going to Aunt Regina's, for "my rest cure." Her mother didn't sleep any that afternoon, and did not make Mavis go to bed early before her company came. She started right away packing Mavis's clothes—cool little shorts and swirly skirts and sleeveless tops. She packed all her summer clothes and two tubes of toothpaste. "We never want to appear cheap," her mother said, when Mavis told her she could use Aunt Regina's.

Three years in a row, when Mavis finished her mother's rest cure with Aunt Regina, she went to her father in Kansas City. He called her Brownie for the tan she'd gotten at Aunt Regina's. He was supposed to have her for the remainder of the summer. For about a week they did city things, and then he left her with the maid in the apartment to watch television and drink red sodas. The maid plaited Mavis's hair in a French braid fresh every day, but after a while, that got tiresome. Finally, the week before school started, she went back to her mother in Texas.

All this took a lot of phone calls and car trips, and as Mavis got older, bus and train rides with her name and destination pinned to her blouse. Mavis watched the frowns on the grownups' faces as they copied down schedules and drew circles over meeting places on road maps. She agreed with her mother: these arrangements for her required so much of everyone's valuable time and money. All except Aunt Regina's. Each summer Aunt Regina made up some excuse to keep Mavis a little longer. As Mavis got bigger, Aunt Regina pointed out that Mavis could swat flies and peel apples and crank the ice cream freezer. And in return, Aunt Regina paid her a penny for every two dead flies, and she didn't mind the extra time Mavis took to peel a whole apple with one long curlicue, and she let Mavis lick the dash.

It seemed like Aunt Regina had a space for her, and Aunt Regina re-did the space every summer so that it was bigger than the summer before. This summer, when Mavis was eight, Aunt Regina said she just *had* to have Mavis the *entire* summer. Mavis was *too* much company and *too* much help to do without.

This summer had started out to be the best one yet for being in love with Root. It began when she got to ride in Mr. Williams' camper, along with his niece and nephew, all the way out to the Panhandle. Aunt Regina had found out Mr. Williams was coming to central Texas and had arranged for her to ride out with him. When Aunt Regina called to propose it, her mother had said, "Oh, what a load that will take off my shoulders." Aunt Regina sent Root along to watch over Mavis.

Every time they stopped, Root came around back and poked his head in. "You all right?" he'd ask. "You want a cold drink, Miss Mavis-Davis?"

Sometimes she'd say she wanted out and lean down and fall into Root's waiting hands. They felt like soft clamps, warm and firm under her arms. He'd set her gently on the ground and she'd trot off to the bathroom. When she came back, she'd put her foot on the bumper and he'd make a little seat for her behind with one hand and boost her up, then give her the Dr. Pepper he'd bought her.

"Thanks, Snoot," she'd say, or Hoot or Shoot, making up a new name for him each stop. She liked to see Root's hair with the little crest in front and a part on the side, not pasted down to his brow by his hat like when he ran the harvester all day.

On this first night of the first whole summer she would spend with them, they sat on the porch after supper, after the floor was swept and the wet tea towels Mavis had used to dry the dishes were spread over the backs of the breakfast chairs to dry.

Mavis cleared her throat. "Root, tell me the story of Dixie." She would ask for nothing but the story tonight.

"Miss Mavis-Davis, you know that story as well as the nose on your face," Root said, waggling his long leg on the banister as he rested his back against a post.

"But I've forgotten some of it." She was sitting cross-legged on the porch floor in front of him.

Root sighed and flicked his toothpick into a bush. "Dixie was born out on the open range in Utah. Her mamma and daddy were from a wild herd of mustangs that was running all over. The man we bought her from says he cut her from her mother's side as a colt." Mavis once winced at this cutting but not anymore. It only meant that Dixie had been separated from her mother by riding between them.

"He ran her into a brush corral, then snubbed her up to a tree three days before she quit kicking. She was a feisty little devil."

"Rupert, watch your language," Aunt Regina murmured from her rocker without looking up from her embroidery.

"Well, she was," he said, pausing.

"Go on! Go on!" Mavis begged.

"The man will always fear the horse"—Mavis chimed in to finish with him—"if the horse doesn't fear the man."

Root laughed. "Mavis, *you* tell *me* the rest of the story."

"So then he fed her sugar until she took the bit and he led her around and finally could climb on her and to this very day she loves a sugar lump best."

"That's right," Root said.

"And she's a mustang paint," Mavis finished.

Two days passed and Mavis could not figure out for the life of her why Root had not asked her to ride Dixie with him. The third evening, she asked the whole thing: Could she ride Dixie by herself? In a way, she hated to give up riding behind Root, remembering other summers how she hugged him around his middle and could feel the warm muscles of his back against her cheek. Still, she must practice alone. An article in the paper said a girl only thirteen had gone on the high wire with her family of acrobats. That was just five years away.

Root laughed. "If Dixie had tires instead of legs, I'd ride her more. She probably won't even let *me* ride her," he said. "I bet I haven't ridden her twice all year." Root had just finished his junior year in high school in town. He and his friend John Don had been riding around a lot in the second-hand pickup Aunt Regina had bought him.

All Mavis could do now was go with Root to the corral in the evenings to feed Dixie her grain. When she felt Dixie's nibbling lips on her palm, a tingling began in her feet and crept slowly up the insides of her legs.

After Dixie finished the grain Root ladled out for her, Mavis watched her take long draughts from the trough, the mare first checking lightly with her muzzle for scum.

Finally, Root would say, "Now you can pet the mustang in 'er," and Mavis would scratch and rub the beautiful prominent bone of Dixie's nose and lay her face against Dixie's strange huge piebald head. Mavis could not think what to do with her longing.

She began to beg and beg so that one afternoon, when a soaking shower had kept the hands out of the fields for the rest of the day, Root put a bridle on Dixie and led her around the corral. At first Dixie chewed the bit and shook her head and leapt sideways, but after a while, she calmed and eventually took the saddle blanket and saddle.

John Don and Mavis watched while Root climbed on Dixie and rode her around the corral and then out into the field. She plodded along indifferently, like the oldest horse in the world, about dead from old age. "No problem. Your turn," Root said, dismounting.

While John Don held the reins, Root helped Mavis put her foot in the stirrup and swing up. She felt the saddle spreading her legs wide. It hadn't been that way when she rode behind Root. It had seemed more circus-y when she could feel Dixie's solid warm rump moving up and down.

Dixie's eyes flared and she shied momentarily, then seemed to settle in her mind that the person atop her was the same one who'd been coming nightly with Root to feed her. Root led her around the corral once, then took his hands away and let Mavis guide her. "So far, so good," he said, more to John Don than Mavis, it seemed.

Next he opened the gate to the inner yard encircling the house and said, "You can ride her around here a little."

Dixie plodded through the gate slowly and Mavis gave her a little goose with the heels of her sandals. At this, Dixie tossed her head and pranced forward a step or two into the yard. She began to dance sideways, first one way and then the other. Mavis looked back at Root.

"Rein her up a little," he called. She pulled sharply on the reins. Dixie half-reared.

"I said a little!" Root called. She heard Root and John Don laugh.

She loosened the reins and Dixie acted as though nothing had happened. Mavis led her across the lawn and began a path around the fence. Dixie was steady, picking up her feet and placing them almost daintily in the lawn grass.

When she thought she was farthest from Root and John Don, Mavis pulled Dixie to a halt.

"What's the matter?" Root called.

Mavis pretended not to hear. She had work to do.

"Give 'er a little spur," John Don called.

Letting the reins go slack, Mavis shook her feet from the stirrups and shucked off her sandals. Dixie put her head down and began eating Aunt Regina's gerbera daisies. Mavis raised her feet and carefully planted them one behind the other on the saddle. Then she stood up.

There was a moment when she was taller than anything else around except the apricot tree. She felt the wind puff out her shorts and fill up her top. It was wonderful, so wonderful. Though she had dreamed it many times, this was her first real time to be a bareback rider. She threw her hands up and out and heard the crowd clapping. Her picture was in the paper. She was captain of the bareback riding team.

In asking for the applause, she forgot she was holding a rein in each hand. When Dixie felt the jerk of the bit, she raised her head from the daisies. That drew her attention to the fact that something had changed atop her. She slung her head and bolted, taking off across Aunt Regina's bachelor buttons and pinks.

The sudden move flung Mavis into the air in a kind of half somersault. For a moment she wondered if she had planned to do this trick anyway. But she came to rest on her back in a pile of duck squat.

"God dammit, girl!" Root sprinted across the drive and entered the yard, catching Dixie as she dashed through the gate. John Don came chuckling and took Dixie's reins.

Root sprinted across the grass to Mavis. "What the hell's the matter with you?" he shouted. "You don't stand up on a horse."

By now she could feel the knot growing on the back of her head and the duck squat soaking her blouse. Root reached down and lifted her up and for an instant she was back at a filling station with Root reaching up into the truck for her. Except this time his hands squeezed her too tight and she couldn't breathe. He set her ajar on her feet, swearing softly as he felt the duck squat between his fingers.

She began to cry. "Go to the house," he commanded. "Now you've got to be doctored like a damned baby. I shoulda' known better."

"Oh Rupert Junior!" John Don called in a high voice over his shoulder as he led Dixie toward the barn. "Your sister's gonna' tan your hide."

In the time before supper, Mavis lay on Aunt Regina's bed with Campho-Phenique on her hands where the reins had cut. "I know you didn't mean to, Dixie," she whispered over and over until she dozed.

Aunt Regina called supper and Mavis hobbled out slowly from the bedroom. Root tousled her hair and held her chair. "The rodeo queen!" he announced. Mavis smiled wanly and took a sip of milk.

When Root had filled his plate, he checked that his sister was occupied in the kitchen. Then he got right into the story for the hands. "Dixie's takin' it real slow and steady around the fence in the yard and the next thing we know she's on the far side of the house and they're stopped." He stuffed a roll in his mouth, chewed twice, took a swallow of tea, and looked at John Don. "We thought Dixie had gone into one of her mustang fits, didn't we, John Don?" John Don nodded, his cheeks puffed with steak.

"But no, it wasn't old Dixie this time, no sirree. It was Mavis here. She stood right up on that horse's back and threw her arms out like she was about to cut the wheat on both sides of 'er."

A ripple of laughter turned into guffaws. Root felt his audience and was winding up to embellish the story when Aunt Regina entered with a refill on rolls. He looked quickly at Mavis. "Isn't that about the way it was, Miss Mavis-Davis?"

Mavis's eyes filled with tears. She tried to sit them out, but they splashed down her front. Finally, she let out a sob and, springing from her chair, stumbled toward the porch.

Aunt Regina looked from Root to John Don and back. "Brother, can't you just leave her be? She's hurting enough." Root took a bite of meat. "I 'spect her backside hurts more'n her feelings right now." And that brought on another spate of laughter while Aunt Regina took Mavis's plate to her on the porch, saying to her that it was cooler and nicer out there anyway, but be sure to come in if the mosquitos get bad.

Alone again, Mavis sat looking at the flies on her food, studying how a girl could start out in the morning going to marry a nice boy with white teeth and by that night hate his guts.

The next day Root tried to make up with Mavis by popping the elastic on the back of her halter.

She drew back. "Don't you ever, ever do that again!" It was what the boys did to a girl when they discovered she was wearing her first bra. She stomped her foot. "Don't you know that's the *worst* thing a boy could do to a girl?"

Root looked at John Don. "The worst, huh?" They laughed.

And from there things just went down.

Days now, days on end, with nothing to do but play alone or help Aunt Regina. Mornings, she gathered eggs, sometimes stroking

Pauline, Aunt Regina's favorite Rock Island layer. When Pauline was sitting on the nest and started to cluck, there was no way she could keep from laying. Mavis raised Pauline's tail to see the egg emerge.

Midmorning Mavis shelled peas, making up a game of speed, or counting each motion. She was good at telling whether to open the pod and run her thumb down the inside to release the moist peas into the steel bowl, or to snap the immature pod into sections. The shelled ones were the older ones, big people who got their way. The snapped ones were babies, with no say-so about when they were picked.

Noons saw the table laden with cabbage, roast, potatoes, squash. Evenings, Aunt Regina would call, "Mavis, honey, come be my legs," and Mavis would trot between the kitchen and dining room, laying out the leftovers—cornbread, cold dabs of vegetables, apple cobbler brought from under the tea towel.

After supper, there was putting away every last dish, sweeping out the kitchen, setting the mouse traps. And finally, to the porch, where she practiced the tight-rope on the railing with Aunt Regina's umbrella until she became shaky and jumped down to sit beside Aunt Regina on the glider and watch the stars burn silver holes in the sky.

Root never touched her now, never engaged her in their silly conversations. He didn't even invite her to go with him in the twilight to feed Dixie. And she was too proud to beg.

One afternoon Root came in early from the field. He bathed and put on fresh jeans that Aunt Regina had ironed nice creases down the legs of. He stood in front of the mirror for a long time combing his hair, making it arch over his white forehead.

Mavis could stand it no longer. She went to Aunt Regina who was setting out peach preserves on the supper table. "Where is Root going?"

"Socializing," Aunt Regina said. "Boys that age like to socialize."

Mavis could not think what that meant. And Root was out the door, leaving behind a sweet smell that reminded her of her mother's boyfriends.

After they had done the dishes, Aunt Regina said she had a headache and believed she would go lie on the day bed with a wet washrag on her forehead.

Mavis went outside and strained to see the black and white spots of Dixie's sides in the corral twilight. The horse was not there. Maybe Root had fed her early. Or maybe he'd totally forgotten her and she was waiting at the gate. Mavis crossed over to the corral but Dixie was nowhere around. She found a feed bucket and turned it upside down to stand on in order to reach the latch on the grain bin. Opening the door, she plunged her hands into the grain. She would touch Dixie's food.

Her motion made the kernels pour down on her, burying her arms up to her shoulders. She climbed up into the little room and sank, half-covered, in the seedy deep. Drawing slow circles, she waded about a while. Then she climbed on a board nailed against the wall and jumped off, landing prettily in the safety net of grain. When she did it again, she acknowledged the crowd far below her. The third time, she did a flip. Maybe, after all, she would be best as a trapeze artist.

Now the kernels filtered into her clothes, eating at the waist of her shorts, filling her panties, making her pockets heavy. She started to sneeze. It was getting dark and Aunt Regina might come looking for her.

As Mavis extricated herself, she heard a scratching noise off to the left. There had been talk at the dinner table of rats this season twice the size of prairie dogs. She jumped wide, banged the door of the bin, and ran for the house, grain trickling out of her clothes.

The next day at noon, she was making a nice pyramid of sliced tomatoes on a pink platter Aunt Regina had let her choose when Root came into the dining room.

"Not yet, Brother," Aunt Regina called from the kitchen. "Y'all wait on the porch. It's cooler and we're running behind today."

Root's face was dark and unsmiling. "I'm here to talk to Mavis," he said. He had never spoken her name like that.

Mavis laid down her knife. "What?"

He stretched across the doorway to the kitchen, resting one hand on the door frame, leaning his face into his sleeve, not entering this women's domain, but not letting anyone escape from it either.

Mavis looked at the dark sweat stain circling his underarm. It made her ashamed to remember she had once liked the smell. He had on the same shirt he had gone socializing in, except now it was wrinkled and the tail hung out.

"You ready for that horse of mine to die?" he said.

"Brother!" Aunt Regina turned, still stirring her gravy.

Mavis swallowed. "Die? What do you mean?"

"You out there at the grain bin last night?"

Mavis picked up her knife and resumed slicing. "So what if I was?"

"Yes or no?" He looked around as if he might spit, then seemed to remember he was inside. He was acting crazy.

"Yes," Mavis said slowly. "I wanted to feed Dixie. You were gone. I thought she was hungry."

"You left the grain bin unlatched," Root said. He paused to see if she might admit it. "Dixie came back in the corral during the night and ate herself sick to death."

Aunt Regina poured the gravy in a bowl. "Oh surely not, Brother."

Mavis took her cue from Aunt Regina. "No big deal, Root the Snoot."

He went on. "You can't let a horse eat their fill of grain and then drink all the water they want. Now she's bloated. She's down out there in the pasture—can't even stand up. Probably dead by tomorrow."

Mavis's eyes filled with tears. She rubbed them with one hand and the tomato juice stung. She dropped her knife and ran from the room.

"Oh Brother," Aunt Regina said, "she's just a child. As for Dixie, it's happened to other horses and they made it through. Must you be so harsh?"

"Probably killed my horse," Root said and turned to go. "You women don't understand nothing."

Mavis lay curled all night beside Aunt Regina, praying, praying for Dixie until she fell asleep exhausted, only to awaken in the pre-dawn with a cold start. She eased off the bed and went out to the porch, sitting down on the top step, pulling her knees against her body under her nightgown. She strained to see out into the darkness.

When things started turning rosy in the morning light, she saw Root walking toward the house.

When he came upon her, his frown deepened. "What you doing up?" He smelled like cigarettes.

"You know," she said, not moving.

Root propped his foot on the step. "You ought to be wondering about Dixie." He spat into the yard.

"I am."

Root popped his knuckles one by one. When he had finished, he said, "Well, little girl. . . ."

Mavis looked up quickly. "Don't call me that!"

"You must not want to know about Dixie very bad."

She looked out from between her fingers. "I do and I don't."

There was a long silence. "She's gone," Root said solemnly, "gone as she can be."

Mavis lowered her head and pressed her eyes into her bony knees. She draped her arms over her head and began to moan.

Root sat down beside her. "You ought to have been more careful, little Miss Mavis-Davis."

"Don't call me that either!" she blubbered.

"Well, it's true," Root said, "and you deserve to be called anything I call you."

"I'm sorry." She began rocking. "I'm sorry, I'm sorry, I'm sor—"

Root rose. "Okay, but just don't ever let it happen again."

She lifted her head. Snot streamed across her lips. "Happen again? How could it happen again?"

A smile, crooked and slow, came to Root's face. "I said she's gone. So where did you think—horse heaven?"

Mavis fisted her eyes. "I—I don't know."

Root took her by the shoulders. "Let this be a lesson, little girl. Lately you've gotten real high-handed and I had to take you down a notch." He gave her a shake. "I said Dixie's gone, but I didn't say where."

Mavis jerked from his grip. "What—?"

He stood back, hands on his hips. "She's gone . . . down to the other end of the pasture." He spat over his shoulder. "She's no dummy. She sure ain't coming back up this way for your poison any time soon."

Mavis gathered her feet under her and stood. She moved slowly backwards across the porch to the door, never taking her eyes off Root. He shoved his hat back and put his thumbs in his front pockets. At the moment she opened the door to go back in to the warmth of Aunt Regina's snoring side, he grinned.

She took a deep breath. "You're not Root, you're rot," she said, and went in.

II. Some of My Best Friends are Relatives

After Long Silence

Have they dreamed their meeting as hand-holding dolls unfolded in an origami family? Call it the prison of kinship. After thirty years, excuses played out, they meet: three women sprung from three Arkansas brothers.

Annie and Jill live in the Bay Area. They have done a few funerals and christenings; otherwise, they stay kin by phone. Today they meet Marie, the visiting Texan, the one who never moved West, young woman.

The Larkspur Ferry landing park. The Californians politely wreathe their Texas cousin. Marie forgets, does a double *abrazo*. Her sprayed hair rebounds from Annie's environmental cheek. Her cream foundation momentarily catches a wisp of Jill's flying brown hair. They stand back for another eyeing. Marie's yellow cotton greets Annie's beige wool, Jill's menswear.

The Californians bring the Texan to heel between them. They stride three abreast, knowing they have only the afternoon.

Up the stairs of the ferry. Dart fore and aft on pretense of finding three seats. Call, beckon one another. Anything to conceal this family voyeurism.

The whistle blows and they set sail across the bay for San Francisco. Marie puts her hood up. "You're cold?" Annie asks. She turns to Jill. "Marie's actually cold."

Annie thinks they should warm their Southwest kin with California wine, comes back sloshing three rosy glasses. A sudden lurch splashes Marie's white tennis shoe. Annie is sorry, so sorry.

69

Marie dismisses it, toasts her wine roughly, like keg draught: "Bonding rites."

Windjammers, and it becomes important to read their names. Soon there's migration to the names of children, spouses, exes: Mandy, Paul, Keith, Suzanna . . . on and on, so many they bob away, toys on the waves.

The Californians point: San Quentin. A block, a huge jutted stone, a place of sealed lips. They recognize the glints in each other's eyes, maximum securities, life sentences yet to be commuted.

Now Alcatraz. Old useless sorrow trapped. Perpetual waves of an inland tide wearing it away, but not in their lifetimes. They are silent, thinking of things back home they plan to forgive but not forget.

The ferry terminal. Disembarking in mid-sentence, the cousins triple off into the little downtown park. People smiling, soaking in the precious sun, nodding and tapping to the jazz trio. Marie lags, lost in the flute. Her cousins indulge her, lighting on the edge of a planter whose flowers they discuss as possibilities for their walkways.

In the elevator at the Hyatt, further indulgences. One must stand away from the glass; one can only stand near it; the third endures all the fuss in bemused silence.

The revolving restaurant sends them into family orbit—mothers and fathers, especially fathers, and other cousins passing in and out of sight like the landmarks of the changing skyline.

"Wait!" the Texas cousin says. "What if there's an earthquake? What do we do?"

"What if?" says Annie. Her ex is an earthquake-stress specialist.

"Scarlett here," says Jill. "I don't think about it."

They order, just for fun, a Honolulu Lulu, a California Lemonade, a Texas Tea. They make rules: When the restaurant completes a quarter turn, retain your straw, slide your drink to the cousin on the right.

"Wow!" the California cousins say, in turn, when they encounter the seven liquors of the Texas Tea. Marie squinches her eyes, shudders at the sweetness of the West Coast drinks.

And their lives . . . a sip of regret here, a gulp of advice there, none willing to drown them all in an afternoon of private sorrow.

They exchange symptoms and remedies of family diseases. Jill received the nerve malady; Marie got the bad guts. They speculate on the chronic depressions of their grandfather, his "blue spells," their grandmother called them. Annie says the area of clinical depression in the left frontal lobe shows up blue on the computer. They toast the prescience of their teetotaling grandmother.

Annie sniffs. "Are you wearing Manly?" she asks Jill. "And if so, why?"

"It's not exactly sex-change surgery. My therapist says it's okay."

"Therapist?" It slips past Marie's lips.

"I've had the same one for eight years now," Jill volunteers. "I nearly croak when she goes on vacation."

Marie can't help it. "Eight years? Lord! Whatever for?"

Annie answers this time. "Self-esteem. Achieving personhood."

Jill shores up the line of defense. "Yeah, Marie, and how are you coping with mid-life?"

Marie looks down toward Market Street. "Everything must curve up," she says in a dream. "And shine. Lips, hair, breasts." She pauses and looks at them. "Psyche too."

They slide their drinks to the right.

Next, it's lost-in-childhoods. The time Jill was literally lost, in Tokyo, at six. The Collie pup lost for a while on the train between Annie's and Marie's. Lost together from their fathers in the Herpetarium in Dallas. These are easy losses to say. But the others: lovers, husbands, children. . .then a sudden recovery to vacations, professions, schedules. But not a single recipe.

High above Market Street, a sweet sadness prowls the downside of the afternoon. The three women gather their things and descend. The boat calls through mist now, and they retrace their steps in alley shortcuts. Two hours ago, strangers passed this way.

Aboard, Annie and Jill wonder if the late afternoon fog will be too much for the Texas cousin. "Nah," Marie says, eager to demonstrate heartiness.

So they find three seats on the open deck, the spray strong and cold when the boat gets underway. They look from one to the other, daring who will chicken out first. Ruined hair? Soaked clothes? Sore throat? No one gives in; stubbornness shines through the genes. Fog blocking out the landscape, they gently turn to politics, compare recent votes, find they are unanimous, give low hoots.

At the landing park, they linger, leaning on their cars to steady their land legs. The fog has moved on, the afternoon turned ancient gold.

Rituals of leave-taking. This time, not the polite yoking of neck and shoulders. This time, the gravity of map and calendar making one body heavy against the other. Enfoldment: long legs matched, belt buckles touching, firm settled breasts in apposition—a reminder that one day they will be each other's only mothers.

A standing back, a promise to write, a quick deft secondary round of embraces. And then they go, back to their places on the earth. Past the chains of family, of ills and sins and maiden names, they have bested themselves.

They are, of all things, friends.

Colors

The wife will drop the assault charges if she can just get her washer and dryer. She already has the rug burns.

As he tells it (he chooses to be his own defense and witness—he happens to know the law like the back of his hand, just in case anyone in the courtroom might be interested), it occurred at the end of a day when he'd worked straight through the afternoon overhauling her brother's engine in the back yard.

He can swear on a stack of Bibles that he drank not more than two six-packs that afternoon—well, maybe a few cans from her brother's supply, but not many. To top it off, it was Valentine's and wouldn't you know, she's gone early that morning so he had to get up and take the kids to school? And late getting home? By the way, she works for a florist.

All he goddamned wanted was a meal. (The defendant is warned about foul language.)

Anyway. She kept going to sleep on the couch. Logical thing was to get her from the couch to the kitchen. Any court of law'd admit that as a good reason. The only means was on her back. She ought to be glad there was a rug. Otherwise, splinters.

He wishes his friend could testify. His friend would of told the truth because the friend was there and saw it all. Rotten system, won't take a man's testimony just because he's a convicted felon.

She took the kids and got hell out to her mother's. In the night, while he was gone just a little while, she came back and hauled off

73

their furniture.

Now, here in this court, like a game show, she is trying for the sunrise gold washer and the avocado dryer he got her at the second-hand store and fixed up good as new.

She testifies. She stood on her feet making Valentine bouquets twelve hours that day. Sick of pink. Sick of red. Couldn't help falling asleep when she got home. Didn't deserve the pink and red rug burns on her back, but for now, just wants the gold and green appliances.

The judge fines him $35 and gives her the washer and dryer. So she can do their children's laundry, the judge tells the jury, who has found the man guilty of assault and battery. The judge has had this guy in here over and over. The fellow doesn't make enough to pay a bigger fine; if he goes to jail, the family won't have the little money he might earn and give them.

Leaving, the husband tells the wife he can't figure what got into her; she used to be loyal to him. His face is getting red. Now she's crazy, hauling him in like this; she don't know what's good for her.

He stops to light a cigarette. His knuckles are white. She moves down the walk. He calls after her, What you want, woman, the rainbow?

How The Neighbors We Never Meet
Move and Leave Us Lonesome

Across the alley, the house is still up for rent, though it's been a year since the people moved. We intended to go over, ring the bell, offer a plate of brownies. We never did.

Once, a woman ahead of me at the postal window gave the address. She was blonde, anorectic-looking. She wore a desperate orange tan and four diamond studs in each ear.

Midnights, there were arguments poolside. Soprano sobs that begged to move back to Mexico City. Guttural answers delivered in thick English: They could not, would not.

Discussed also were his unfaithfulness, her nervous condition, their miraculous son. How they shouldn't get this drunk. And things, always things that would never work out. This lasted through summer. In the fall, a moving van.

But the man and the woman left remembrances. A white-hot security light that comes on at dusk and illuminates our bedroom like the eye of God. A poolside phone braying like a jackass night after night.

When it begins to ring, we awaken and lie holding hands, listening to its cry and trying to make sense of the patterns of white light on our walls.

I say, "Some night I'd like to climb that fence and answer that phone."

You say, "Maybe it would be them, just checking on things."

So I practice. "Hello?" I say. "No one's home." I pause. "Oh, hi there—it's *you*!"

Going Forth

"You are the winner of our discontent." Irv was careful to cross the T's in "discontent." He didn't want Helene to think he was a sicko. Though the marriage was kaput after 41 years, he could extend him-self this last time, give her the gift of a little pun. Would she remem-ber seeing the movie together, that it had starred Donald Sutherland and Tuesday Weld? He smiled as he read over the note, signed it "Me," and folded it once.

Helene would be back in an hour. She would come in puffing, her face glistening, her bulky exercise shoes thumping across the hallway. Before she got to the bathroom, she would have her shirt off. She would have noticed his car wasn't there and presumed he'd gone out for a gizmo at the hardware store.

Maybe, because he wasn't there, she would hum in the shower. It might be an hour before she discovered the note on the dining room table. By then he'd be safely gone.

He jerked open his underwear drawer, saw immediately the reason he was leaving. His socks were grouped in blacks, browns, and whites. Yes, that was exactly why, right there, he had chosen to go. He clutched a handful of black, another of white, leaving all the brown. Brown was the fashion choice of old men. Revelations were coming to him right and left this morning. It was all very clear from the moment he opened his eyes, like he could see again after a long but reversible blindness.

Once a man in a bar had told him a story of falling down a flight of stairs at the state school for the blind. The tumble had literally opened the man's eyes, so after that there really wasn't any reason to be at the blind school and they made him leave. Crazy, wasn't it? But then life was like that.

In the garage, Irv loaded into the trunk a duffel bag with a jumble of underwear, socks, ties. Cuff links clinked in the bottom against the cleats of his golf shoes.

He would show Helene. Eighteen holes of golf every day and he would enjoy it like never before and wouldn't think of her. After all, he was retired and he could do what he wanted, exactly what pleased him. He'd kept up her and the kids all these years. Now he was retiring from that too.

Irv's company had asked him to retire at 60 and he'd said gladly. At first he'd watched television all day, just to see what everyone was talking about on the soaps and the sleaze talk shows. Then he'd built some odds and ends at his workbench.

He would try to forget the hurt he experienced when Helene had refused to go with him to the club in the afternoons and play bridge with the other wives. That hurt him deeply, he might have told her. But Helene was so preoccupied, so into her own thing, like getting her 3,000-hour pin as a hospital volunteer, and taking literature appreciation at the local junior college, and that fool aerobic class three times a week. Disgusting, how she couldn't bring herself to settle down with him.

There had been a time, much earlier in the marriage, when she was there to serve drinks to him and his golf buddies when they came off the greens. The cocktail napkins with golfer cartoons. Never forgot the swizzle sticks, not once.

Yes, that was *exactly* why he was leaving—Little Miss Perle Mesta, Killer-With-Kindness, Angel May . . . but here he got all mixed up. He had started out to think he was leaving her because she wouldn't go with him to the club, and he'd ended up thinking it was because she was once too sweet.

And now? Now she would call out, "There's beer in the fridge."

He remembered the instant last night when he knew he definitely would go, a moment totally clear to him, that he not only *would*, he *must*. It was the only way to redeem their lives. Otherwise, he might kill her outright, as she was killing him slowly, day by day.

He had been closing the bathroom door when it dawned on him as a distinct possibility. By the time he was naked and had the right water temperature for his shower, he was sure. When he pulled up the button to the shower, he felt the resolve surge through him as the water spurted out. And he said to himself that in the life to come—if he had ten or twenty more years—he would mark his new life by this moment of self-baptism.

James might tease a bit. "Couldn't you make up your mind, Dad, after 41 years?" Then James would go on about his business being a loan officer in a bank across the country. James could be as tight-lipped about his feelings as he was about his bank's assets.

Jane would say, "For heaven's sake, Dad, what kind of example is that to set for David and me? You think we want to get married if you and Mother can't make a go of it?"

And Irv wouldn't know what to say back to his own grown daughter, who'd been living with her significant other for seven years already with never a peep about tying the knot.

Helene would weep copiously. She might even take to her bed. She would call her friends and they would agree that all men are despicable worms—all except their own sons, of course, for they hadn't the slightest idea in what category to place them.

Then Helene would wake up the third morning and call the bank to find out if Irv had taken all their money out of checking and emptied their lockbox. He would not give her that satisfaction.

Now, coming back into the house, easing the screen door quietly out of habit these past few months, he noticed his throat had filled up with some kind of crud. First he spat into a tissue, but then he had to go in the bathroom and spit into the toilet. Was it possible to get cancer of the throat in one morning?

Maybe it was psychosomatic. Helene would say so. She might quote her psychology book from last semester, get out her notes and read to him, beginning with "Listen to this, honey."

Originally they had loved each other. She wore her hose seams straight and had a tiny waist. When he came home from Korea, he had been handsome in his Navy uniform and had grown a cute mustache. She had worked as a secretary until he was discharged and then they did what you did: had a baby. And then another.

Those times were filled with something lost now. He had worked hard and Helene had been a good mother. Sometimes then, he had thought the loneliness of his life was permanently erased, especially when he held one of the babies in the air and a tiny drool streamed down on him. "Bingo!" he'd say, and the baby would startle and they'd laugh.

Then he would think—or maybe not even think—but the idea passed over him some way: This is what it means to be perfectly happy. Now Helene had ruined that picture, utterly.

They even took a cruise to the Bahamas for their twenty-fifth wedding anniversary. She had been so thrilled, had rushed out and bought a little sunsuit of a thing with an anchor on the front, had gotten him a sailor hat. He could still picture her now on the deck of the ship, that silly passion flower tucked over one ear.

All this made Irv think of their little coffee travel kit and he went into the kitchen to find and take it. He began to open and close the cabinet doors, glancing briefly at the dishes, anger rising at how neatly she kept all the similar glasses in a group, the bowls stacked in graduated sizes, as if it was a big deal. Who did Helene think she was, anyway, lording her mindless little household expertise over him?

Irv was not going to feel one pang of guilt in taking the coffee kit, not one. After all, he was leaving her the house. And there were many other good things, acts of kindness and deeds of mercy on his part. He was, as the phrase went, a thoroughly good family man. Braces on the kids' teeth—no small expense; summer camp; a brand new car for Helene every third year.

He found the coffee kit and refilled the little jar with instant coffee from the larger one, spilling a few grains on the counter top. Thinking with satisfaction how she would have no cause to fault him for making a mess, he cleaned it up carefully. In the early days, she had lovingly, silently cleaned up the messes that happened when he was in a hurry.

One more of these little kitchen-type messes: really, the thing with Trudy was only that. Trudy came to work in his office and only a month passed before he knew he was on Trudy's wanted list. Looking back, he didn't know what he saw in her except she had terribly long legs, made even longer by the short skirts and high heels she wore each day. And the way she said all her "v's" as "w's" like the time he bit her thigh gently and she laughed her guttural laugh and said, "Oh Irw, don't you get wiolent on me."

Gradually, he fell into something with her that started with an "l"—love or like or lust—now he couldn't say what. The man he was back then puzzled him. He constantly asked him to come out of the fog.

Meanwhile, Helene just got happier and happier with the two kids he'd given her. In fact, although she did everything for him like always, he began to wonder where her heart was, and if it was big enough for him anymore, what with her happiness over the kids.

So he had taken Trudy's legs out of loneliness for someone to love him like he should be loved. He had taken the rest of her too, and repeatedly, until Trudy's husband found out and came one night to their door threatening to kill him.

After the man had gone (Irv had appealed to him quietly, veteran to veteran, backing him out to the front steps) Irv was so shaken he told Helene everything, blurting out that Trudy's only attraction had been her legs, seductively displayed. Really, Trudy had made a fool of herself over him. Could he help it if he was attractive to other women?

After Helene had thrown his things quietly about the bedroom, he offered his arms to her and she allowed herself to be drawn against him and she sobbed a while.

He had thought she'd gotten the crying out of her system that night but no. She went on weeping night and day. Her crying—it was probably deliberate—made him miserable. He had apologized, damn it, and why couldn't she just accept that and forget it? Other women

81

did. Well, this last he didn't know for a fact but he thought so, surely.

She carried on so long he began to feel justified in his indiscretion, realizing he'd married someone so weak, so inferior, and numbingly simple-minded that she could not take any of life's little everyday problems.

The marriage counselor told him in his private session that unless he abjectly apologized, appeared totally at fault, he might lose everything—his wife, house, children, job, and his good name. "That's the way this fooling around works," the guy said, leaning back in his chair, hands behind his head, grinning and rocking in small nervous jerks. The little punk ought to know: he'd been married three times himself.

So Irv had done that, scared to death she would get their stock signed over or tell the children or put all his clothes in the front yard.

And she had done none of those things. Just cried, cried for days and nights on end. After they'd gone to bed at night, she'd ask, "Why? Why would you do such a thing to me?" He finally had to tell her the nights were not the time to talk. And no, his evening TV was not the time—he deserved a little peace and quiet. Meals were definitely out because of the children.

God, how he hated all her women's magazine articles clipped and laid on his nightstand to read, her insistence that they keep going to the insipid little therapist week after week.

Now the stuff was filling his mouth and he had to stop every five minutes or so from cleaning out his desk and go into the bathroom to spit. He began to see how this rising in the gorge had to do with Helene. She was causing this thing, the very thought of the way she had acted over the years. By God, she wouldn't make him literally sick. He would get away from her kind of poison before that happened.

The therapist suggested all kinds of possible problems in their marriage but really, neither of them could come up with much. Of course, there were silences at times. Of course, she didn't always come to the door to meet him when he came home. (If she had, she would have smelled Trudy's perfume on him earlier than the night

Trudy's husband came.) But neither one could think of what they had done to deserve Irv's infidelity and so gradually, they let it drop.

Yes, Helene remained angry for months but she only threatened divorce the first month because, as she said later in a calm moment, "You have my health insurance and you are the father of my children."

In a way, he had been hoping for more. Although he told her he loved her and only her—and he guessed he did, it made him ache all over that she would take him back. For it meant he had to measure up. She took away his tragedy with her acceptance. She made him miserable with her strength.

Now there was a cold civility about them that threatened to wreck him. He wanted to rage at her for going on like nothing had happened. Funny, he'd noticed recently for the first time that he could not tell what she was thinking. How long this had been going on, he couldn't say. Probably years before he quit work. She smiled mysteriously and often did not bother to start a conversation.

There had been a Saturday afternoon, long ago, in a summer when the children were away and not long after the Trudy thing, when Helene had begun to cry quietly when they finished making love. He let her talk some then. . .about how she loved him, how she knew she was foolish but she was a one-man woman, how she wanted their marriage to grow and grow but they had to work on it.

He had let her talk until she ran down. And then he stroked her hair and told her quietly he didn't think a marriage should be worked on, like an extra bedroom and bath being added to a house.

She asked, "The thing is, how do I know you've changed? How?"

He had been proud of his answer. Taking her face in his hands, squeezing her cheeks ever so slightly, and with his face close to hers, he had said, "Trust: that's what it's all about. You have my word; if you won't take that, I have nothing more to offer."

Her eyes had grown wide. "But—"

He never let her finish. "No buts." And then he'd made a definition. "Marriage," he said in a voice designed to be both magnanimous and authoritative, "is comfort. You either have it or you don't."

Then he'd asked her, very reasonably, if she could be through with *the* problem. If, please, for his sake and if she really loved him, they could lay this thing to rest forever. She promised with all her heart to try. And she did.

So what gave her the right to be so goddamned cocky? Who gave her the keys to the kingdom? What man wouldn't do it again in the face of a wife that trotted right on with her life, deliberately making him miserable?

Trudy's husband had of course made her quit immediately and two or three young empty-headed girls had come and gone, but that was during the time he'd had the scare with his colon polyps and had finally had to have them removed, and that would have been a real turn-off to any of them, so it was just as well they were bimbos.

Then Sharon came. She was thirty and had been married once upon a time. He missed Trudy's long legs but Sharon had breasts that sure beat Trudy's fried eggs. She was lonely and available. Irv made sure, the very first day of her coming into the office, that she didn't have a husband. He was no fool.

Sharon told him once in bed that she loved the way his hair was thinning on top, that she'd never trust a man with a full head of hair. Did he snore after he and Sharon made love, the way Helene let him know he did in the night by patting him to get him to turn over? Come to think of it, it didn't matter one bit because this wonderful girl got right up and brewed coffee, then sat quietly in the living room in a pink-flowered kimono until he'd recovered himself enough to struggle out and have a cup with her before he went home to Helene's supper.

Helene would never sit with him and have coffee. He had to admit he had asked her to leave him alone in the mornings, said he needed to concentrate on his paper—but that was mornings. At night, when she could certainly have been there for him, at least during commercials, she sat reading her literature book, nodding and marking passages.

Cleaning out his desk wasn't too hard. He determined to take a few things he'd brought home from the office—the booklet "Planning

Retirement Happiness," his thirty-year gold desk set, the card signed by everyone in the office—and stuff that would be no good to Helene and the kids—his army commendation, social security card, passport, and a keepsake book of his parents' war ration stamps.

The thing with Sharon on Saturdays would have been fine if the wife of one of his golfing buddies hadn't asked Helene why Irv wasn't playing golf anymore on weekends with the group. Then Helene had done a mean, sneaky thing. She'd gone out to his golf bag and snapped a small piece of plastic wrap in the flap of the compartment that held his favorite iron. When he came home from Sharon's that afternoon, she showed it to him, still in place. "You didn't play golf today, did you?" she said coldly.

His heart thudded in his ears and his breath came shallow. Black spots winked all over the garage. "Sure I did," he said.

"I think not," she said, and turned and went inside. He'd stumbled in, blubbering something about intermittent rain. In the bathroom, he'd regrouped and come out to tell her he'd tried out someone else's irons, thinking he might buy the set off the man.

She was drawing a meat loaf from the oven. "I don't believe that for one minute," she said, never taking her eyes off the dish. That was what just killed him, the way she didn't take her eyes off the meat loaf.

So that night, when he could stand it no longer, he came clean about Sharon. Helene sat impassively through his confession, then said, "What's she like this time?"

"She was lonely," Irv said lamely. "Her father was killed in an accident. I don't think she had anyone." Of course he didn't mention that Sharon was the same age as their daughter, or that she had wonderful boobs.

This time there was no crying in his presence. He slept in the guest room for a month, creeping in after the children were salted away in their rooms for the night. But he could hear her crying after he'd left their bedroom. In the daytime she acted normal, if a little cool, and she never suggested the therapist, or went to see her sister, or left off cooking his meals.

When she had asked, "Is this all, these two?" he had said yes, and by God, that was the truth. And it had remained the truth, even though, since then, he had slept briefly with a half-dozen more. But they were not really affairs, just afternoons.

For a long time after that, maybe two years, he'd spent every waking moment accounted for. His weekends were infernally long, puttering in the yard. He made berms and tore down berms. He estimated he had moved every square foot of dirt on that lot at least once, some twice. He went into outdoor cooking, building a brick grill with a chimney. Finally Helene suspected she had an ulcer from too much charred meat and asked him to slow down on the cookouts.

When he had been working every day, he had been able to put her and her everlasting activity out of his mind. He had never noticed how she cooked extra and took food to sick neighbors or their friends who had people coming for a wedding or a bar mitzvah. There was no pinpointing exactly when he'd first noticed her doing this, but it seemed she had at least stepped it up right after the Sharon blowout.

Why did her do-gooder business make him uncomfortable? God knows he approved of helping people. It was just that, well, friends and sometimes even perfect strangers got more of her attention than he did. No, that wasn't quite right: she always had his meals for him. It was something about the way she got kind of excited when she was cooking for someone else. They loomed up big in her mind, and he did not.

Now the stuff in his mouth came continually and he went straight to his handkerchiefs in the bedroom chest. They were in two neat stacks, white and colored. He took a white one and spat into it, crumpled it, and laid it on top of the chest. He realized he had forgotten his handkerchiefs when he collected his underwear. He snatched up the entire batch, crushing them in a huge fistful, making sure they were mixed.

A brief, scary vision came to him of her helping him with one of the colored ones, making an ascot for his throat, learning how to clean the hole in his throat, learning quickly and expertly how to close the hole with her hand so he could speak. He would be fumbling, just fumbling for the flap, and she'd reach over and press his throat with her fingers so he could croak out a few syllables. Through Helene, and at her pleasure, he would communicate with the rest of the world.

He got an old shopping bag from the back of her closet and hurled the handkerchiefs into it. The bitch would never control him like that. He'd die in a rented room, with nobody there, before he'd let her take care of him.

On top of that, her hair had started to turn gray and she had left off her hair coloring. It was a shame. Why should he put up with that for twenty more years?

Funny he had never noticed that his shirts were always hung facing the same direction, and they were separated into dress and casual. How long had she been doing things like this? He wanted to kill her.

Yes, that was it. He was leaving before he killed her outright some morning just after she'd poured him more coffee and asked if he'd like a second bran muffin. Otherwise, yes, he would strangle her with his two bare hands, take her down there in the kitchen, her fluffy pink houseshoes flung out as she struggled briefly, the only evidence of violence beside her lifeless form in the pink housecoat when they came to take him away.

He began to sort his clothes, arranging and rearranging in categories. He said aloud: "These she can throw away; these she should give to the Salvation Army; these she can take to the cleaners."

And what was the motive? they would ask. He would say sadly and with conviction, "It was self defense." They wouldn't buy that.

"She tried to be my mother." That sounded downright ridiculous. Even he knew that wasn't true.

"She was trying to save me." There. That was better.

The phone rang. "Oh, for God's sake!" he said, not knowing if he said it for catching himself in the silliness of planning what would happen to his clothes after he left, or the irritation of the interruption. He glanced at the clock. She would be back in thirty minutes.

"Hello Irv, how's it going?" Marilyn said.

He cleared his throat, and then a second time. "Fine, just fine."

"You don't sound too good. Catching a cold?"

"Just a frog."

"Hearing you say frog reminds me of something I read in the paper last night. Did you know in merry old England, people dangled live frogs down their throats to cure themselves of sore throats?"

He might kill Marilyn too. "I don't have a sore throat. It's just that I haven't spoken to anyone for a couple of hours."

Marilyn laughed. "That must mean your social secretary isn't there."

These middle-aged women cute-sies drove him absolutely crazy. "If you mean Helene, no, she's not here," he said dryly.

Marilyn pressed on. "Then maybe you could say. Max and I are having a few couples from the hospital volunteers over for coffee and cake next Wednesday evening. Do you know of any reason you two couldn't come?"

If he told Marilyn the reason he knew of, it would send a shock wave from here to Japan. "I'll tell her and she can call you," he said instead.

"I'll bet you're loving your retirement. Max wishes he were in your shoes." Marilyn hadn't seemed to hear his reply. The crap was building up in his throat again.

"I'll tell Helene. Thanks, Marilyn." He banged the phone in its cradle. Maybe Marilyn would think he was getting old and hard of hearing. He forgot he'd been sorting his clothes and went now to the bathroom cabinet.

He looked blankly at a few pill bottles with his name on them—a muscle relaxant, something for migraines he'd had years ago, a pain reliever the doctor had sent him home with when his polyps were removed—Helene could use those for her hemorrhoids. He remembered how a flare-up of hers kept them from going to the beach one summer weekend. That was another thing; she was always changing their plans, purposely keeping him from having fun.

A mountain climber on TV last night said it all, "Life is mutable. If you want to climb a mountain, you've got to do it today." Irv had gone straight and looked up "mutable."

He got the shopping bag with the handkerchiefs in the bottom and tossed in the pill bottles, a blue tin of laxative pills, and a large bottle of antacid with crust around the lid. When he reached for the vitamins he remembered they were joint property. She took hers every day. He took one when his golf game was off. She could have them, for he wouldn't be feeling bad at all once he was out from under her control.

His shaving kit with razor and toothbrush were next, with the toothpaste magnanimously left behind. That was something he could pick up at a drugstore. Should he begin a list?

Looking at his collection of cologne, several unopened from past Christmases, he chose a large green bottle shaped like a crown. It slipped from his fingers as he was putting it in his shaving kit and crashed to the tile counter. The contents dripped over the edge and the whole room was suffused with "King."

Irv grabbed a towel and sopped, pinching the bits of glass into the towel at the same time. Just as he got it controlled, he sneezed and his nose began to run. He left the ball of towel on the counter, mainly because he couldn't think what to do with it. Helene would be surprised when she started to put it in the laundry in her too-efficient way and the glass sprayed out. Then maybe she would hate him. He hoped so.

Now the odor of King came back to him on a waft of air conditioning and he realized it would permeate the whole house. When she came in the door, she would wrinkle her nose and say, "What's that smell?"

Standing over the toilet, spitting, blowing his nose with toilet paper, he remembered a story from the newspaper (he'd read all of it every day since his retirement) telling what you ought to do if your nose suddenly began to run copiously. It was a sign your spinal fluid had broken through your nasal passages. You were to lie down and call 911. Or was it get someone to take you to the ER? Or hell, did it really matter which way? For it was dangerous and all might be lost, literally. Would he be paralyzed or would his brain be as dry as a buffalo chip or just what?

That's all he needed, to lie whimpering in a hospital bed while Helene stood over him assuring him she loved him and would take care of him. She would go home in the evenings from the hospital, and later from the nursing home, and she would be happy as a lark in that empty house.

Once, when she was working on the marriage, she insisted they say goodnight to each other and kiss, even when they were not going to bed at the same time. She had wanted at least a kiss and she woke him up crying more than once when she found he had turned in while she was in the basement folding laundry. (To tell the truth, most of those times he had been extra tired after an afternoon with Trudy or Sharon or one of the others that didn't really count.) He had held Helene in his arms tenderly, letting her cry herself out, feeling the nobility of his patience.

Now she had turned the tables. At ten the house might grow silent, and Irv, climbing the stairs from his workbench, would find her already asleep, his little bedside light glowing cheerfully for him. He hated her most of all then. She did not seem to care anymore. Yes, *that* was why he was leaving.

He liked it better, the more he thought of it, almost any other time than now, when she was so recovered. Looking at her calm—even happy chopping celery or writing letters to her college roommate—he daydreamed of the years she had cried so hard, had needed his arms and his asking for forgiveness. These times seemed preferable to the gentle equilibrium that had come over her, the smugness, as though she'd managed secret sessions with a new therapist. Now he was as important to her as one of her better living room chairs.

Irv stood and blew his nose until he filled the commode with toilet paper and as he flushed, he hoped it wouldn't clog. Then he remembered he wouldn't be there to deal with it. Good enough for her if it did. Maybe she'd appreciate him more when she had to deal with these home maintenance problems.

Her and her feminist ideas. He turned now toward the garage, checking to see how his time was. Fifteen minutes to gather his fishing gear. There was a circle of oil in the garage where her car usually sat. Sooner or later, she'd have to have a ring job. She probably didn't even know what to call it, might even challenge Joe, their car repairman after he'd made the diagnosis.

He picked through his rods and reels—no use taking but the best. Choosing two, he marveled that their lines were loose. He spent a few minutes untangling them, cursing softly when a hook imbedded itself briefly in his finger. He hadn't fished for years but he planned to, damned often.

She'd probably buy herself a new car instead of getting this one fixed. Helene was like that now. You couldn't tell her a thing. When they were newlyweds, she'd say, after he'd explained how the stock market worked or the difference in kinds of life insurance, "You know everything!"

And when the children were little, she had been so busy being their damned happy mother she'd at least accepted it when he said they didn't need a new hot water heater, or had to move from here to there, or were trading in her car even though she liked it. In the early days, all he'd had to say was, "Are you challenging me?" and she'd shrink back to her place.

Now she still wouldn't argue. But she'd come home, like as not, saying she'd been looking at cars with an eye to trading hers in. The truth was, she'd have the deal all signed, sealed, and delivered.

He collapsed the fishing poles and threw them in the trunk, loading his tackle box after them. It came as a shock that there was still so much room in his trunk; he expected his car to be overflowing by now. Wasn't his past life at least a carful?

Oh yes, his clothes back in the house. Comforted, he went in and took a while to determine which of his shirts would look all right not ironed; he would leave the rest. Lately, some of his golfing shirts with stretch bands around the waist had been a struggle to get into. He selected five straight-cut knit ones.

Helene had dieted down to her first-married weight just to spite him. Still, her upper arms were beginning to sag, regardless of how many times a week she went to her aerobics workout. Not long ago, she had gleefully pointed out that she was wearing some jeans Jane had left behind. That, he had wanted to say, is obscene, an embarrassing fact for the wife of a retired man, even if her legs were long and skinny. Besides, the jeans did not match her neck, which was definitely beginning to wrinkle.

It didn't much matter which clothes he took. He was going to buy a whole new wardrobe when he got settled. Helene had gotten most of his clothes for him, bringing home at one whack three ties, six shirts, four pairs of pants—carefully preserving the sales slip and sack so she could return the ones he didn't like. He had taught her to do that back when he was working so hard for the family.

Now his time was up and Helene would be home any moment. He raced across the house toward the garage, his arms loaded, scooping up the shopping bag with his handkerchiefs and toiletries on the way. All was quiet in the garage. Where was she anyway?

Then he remembered. She had told him earlier but in his distraction he had forgotten. She was going to the library after aerobics. It was the genealogy society's morning. Helene had been thinking of tracing her family's history. She had talked about it way too much, bored him to death at times when she found a cousin in a phone book of some city they were visiting. Of course, it was *her* family, not his, not the name their children bore. This was typical of her selfishness.

Okay, so he had a reprieve. He got his bowling ball from the den closet. The case was coated with light pink mildew. There were even limits to Helene's compulsive cleanliness. Years since he'd bowled. Were any from his bowling league still in town? Put on the list: look up Sam and Bill (Maxine too!!)

Ball to the car, head like a ball, throbbing. Not a loss of spinal fluid. A brain tumor instead. He went to the kitchen and gulped four aspirin, considering briefly whether he might die of an overdose. It would serve Helene right for the way she was killing him. Spitting in a paper towel and chucking it across the room, he missed the trash can and left it there. His head pulsed angrily.

There were two more things he wanted. The drawer in the den with all the family pictures was hopelessly stuffed. He slammed the drawer shut and went to their bedroom where he took Jane's and James' pictures in their gold frames. They were their college graduation pictures, James with a green tassel for English, Jane with blue for business.

By God, he had seen his family through. It hadn't been easy. It was something he could be awfully proud of. He considered for a moment slipping the pictures out, leaving the empty frames for Helene to see what she had done to the family. It would make the loss of the pictures more noticeable, but then he decided to take them in their frames. After all, he'd just have to buy some more, wherever he was.

He opened the drawer to his nightstand and took out his handgun. He had never had to use it, thank God. Now he might, someplace. It felt too hard and cold in his hand. Had he ever had a carrying case for it? It would look strange in the top of the shopping bag. If the police stopped him for some reason, there it would be. He put it back in the drawer. Helene might need it; she would be all alone. Be decent.

He closed the drawer and left the room with the pictures. That was it. There for a minute he had softened. The gun had brought to mind life and death. He reminded himself that he was leaving in order to save the lives of everyone in the family. He was no madman loose with a gun. Let Helene shoot *him* if she wanted to.

Glancing at the clock, fifteen minutes left. A walk through each room, thinking what he might have forgotten, how he would never again see these rooms, how she could finally arrange them exactly as she chose. In the kitchen he took an apple and a banana from the bowl on the counter. He was entitled to a snack. When he started to set the alarm, he dropped the apple and it rolled under the breakfast table. He left it there to show the turmoil he was in as he left.

In the car, three deep breaths. "I hope you're satisfied," he said aloud. What would he say to her if he met her in the driveway: "Be right back"? He did not want a confrontation. God knows she had staged plenty of those in the nights of crying and begging him to talk to her.

He drove to the entrance of the subdivision and read backwards over the iron entryway, for the last time, Meadow Acres. Neither a meadow nor acres. He looked both ways carefully, and when he had the right-of-way, he discovered a decision was necessary: left or right. He sat there a full minute. Where to go first? The car behind him honked.

Helene would be coming in from the left. He jerked out to the right and drove a mile, then pulled over on the grassy shoulder. He would have to think a minute to decide where he was going. He opened the car door and spat, hitting a daisy dead-eye.

It's Almost Sad

They were a Southwest couple.

He was a gardener of sorts, pulling weeds and stray grass out of his beds at night while their chili bubbled. The beds were Southwest beds, filled with red rock and black lava, Mexican heather, sedum, aloe, and cacti, especially cacti.

She worked as an exercise instructor but had a side business in her own pretty hair—long, strong, light brown. It did things she wanted it to—lay down, stood up, puffed, jiggled. Every day was a good hair day for this woman.

The gardening man and the hairful woman declared their love every few days and were actually happy for a while.

Inevitably, one day the man asked, Is this all there is in life? He redid his flower beds, replacing the moss rose—too sentimental, with widelia, a coarser ground cover. He added whiskey barrels and wood chips. He left his cactus right where it was.

I yearn for fulfillment, the woman said. She bought new hair products for volumizing and shining and bouncing and, for good measure, calming split ends she might not have detected. She did not cut her hair.

They began to think thoughts. She thought he spent too much time with his garden. It was unnatural, unmanly. Besides, he never grew roses. Even if he had, even if he had given them to her, they wouldn't have counted toward love. For they would not have been expensive.

He thought she was entirely too vain about her hair. He suspected she was primping for someone at the exercise club. Maybe she should cut her hair and just leave it alone? Yet, if she cut it, such an act would definitely be spiteful. She knew how he loved long hair.

By working hard at unhappiness, they were able to make life more interesting. When the man left the house in the morning, he thought, She doesn't even turn off the hair dryer when I kiss her goodbye.

Later, when the woman left, she looked sadly at his new plantings. He cares more about his rocks and flowers than he does me.

One evening, when TV was even more boring than their lives, they decided to break up. Each one felt the power of another out there somewhere, a person or persons unknown now calling to them.

At the last minute they hesitated. They were supposed to seek counseling. Next day she talked to her girlfriend at the exercise club. He talked to his friend in the office down the hall. Both concurred it was all over. To separate was best.

That night they drove through the alleys to collect cardboard boxes.

The next night, after work, he dug up his prize cactus, hefted it into a big box and placed the box atop his other things in the bed of his pickup.

She stood a while in the bathroom brushing her hair, asking soul-searching questions of the woman in the mirror. On the toilet behind her sat a large box of hair-enhancing materials.

Saying goodbye out front, they agreed on a hug, a light kiss. At the last minute, the wind blew her hair across her mouth, too late for him to abort his motion toward her. His lips touched the strands glommed to her lips. Damned hair!

Now she shrieked. In his embrace, he had pressed her with cactus spines stuck to his sleeve. Porcupine lover!

They went to their cars, heads bowed. Of course it was over. There had been signs. These were the final straws, literally.

And just to think—if they had been happy? Well, you and I both know we would not have had much of a story.

Coming Clean

"Underbody Wash" and "Rustbuster" are dirty words to Lee. "Wheelbrite" sets her teeth on edge and "Orbital Buff" sounds like a cosmic striptease.

Lee has been afraid of automatic carwashes as long as they have existed. Her father always washed the family car on Saturday afternoons in the driveway with a bucket of soapy water and a running hose. Her husband Jim is liberated. He laughs and says, "You drive your car. You wash it."

Lee tells him she is jinxed, that carwashes have something against her. She can tell carwash stories like other people tell scary airplane stories. She even cried a little in the evening after the day her windshield cracked in the carwash, zigzagging right in front of her when the water hit the glass. Well, hell, she couldn't help it if it was 94 degrees that day and she had to go to the mall for a couple of hours first.

"How was I to know not to run the air conditioner? Don't I get to *breathe* inside a car wash?"

"Common sense tell you something?" Jim asked.

"Tell me what?"

"Extreme sudden hot or cold can break glass."

"Yeah. Okay. But I *still* think the carwash has a contract out on me. Maybe from now on. . ."

Jim rose from the table and began clearing the dishes. "Sorry, I do dishes and bills. I don't wash other people's cars."

So now Lee waits as long as she can, and when the glass is bug-spattered and the doors so dirty she is smudged getting in and out, she goes to the E-Zee Wash.

Certainly it isn't a phobia, though her throat feels tight and her heart beats wildly when the man takes her money and says, "Don't steer turn off your windshield wipers don't put your foot on the brake put it in neutral check all your windows don't drive off until the signal go ahead now."

When the belt jerks her into the spray, she turns up the tape and hums with James Taylor. As the soap squirts on, she thinks of herself at the Monterey Bay Aquarium, about to look at the demonstration of ocean tides in the glass before her.

But when the giant blue octopus descends, its strips of carpet jiggling a few inches from her nose, she rests her head on the wheel. Stingrays and man-o'-wars close in from the sides and churn past. About the time she is sure she has been targeted by aliens, there is an ominous pause.

Now comes the Arm of Doom. Full of tornadic wind, the dryer thuds down on the windshield.

The car jiggles, then plummets from the opening. Towel-flipping, joke-telling boys descend. Sixty seconds later, the loud "Thunk! Thunk!" on the trunk—a disdainful pat on the back-side?—signals they are finished. Lee puts the car in gear and is history, forgetting, always forgetting, she will skid on her wet tires as she pulls onto the street.

But Lee is working on it, the whole sorry secret of her carwash fright, and today she has lined up an ally to help her deal with it.

"Have you ever been through a carwash?" Lee casually asks her neighbor, Mrs. Fort, who sits beside her in the car. Mrs. Fort needs a ride home from her standing appointment, so Lee has swung by the beauty shop on her way from work.

Everything about Mrs. Fort is neat, including her white wavy hair, now carefully shampooed and set for the week, along with the neat-pressed slacks she wears with flowered or plaid tops. Mrs. Fort thinks it's an interesting coincidence that her age and weight are the same this year, 92—a little joke on herself she has shared with her neighbors.

For she is still capable of bringing a plate of brownies to a household whose mother has the flu. And she continues to get out her mower and begin on her yard—until someone looks out the window and sends a teenager to gently wrest the mower from her gloved grip. After an appropriate protest, Mrs. Fort disappears into the house to provide a glass of fresh limeade for the worker.

Now Lee and Mrs. Fort turn in to E-Zee Wash and idle behind two cars until their turn. Lee guides the car into the tracks, rolls down the window and gives the man his money, rolls up the window, double-checks it, then puts the car in neutral.

She looks at Mrs. Fort. "We don't have to do another thing," she says. "These carwashes are great. We just sit back and enjoy the rain."

They have barely gotten inside when Lee becomes aware that something has gone dreadfully wrong. With the first gush of soap, Mrs. Fort jumps and looks at her arm. With the second, she puts her hands to her newly coifed hair. Soapy water is streaming down on Mrs. Fort.

Lee clicks her seat belt loose and lunges toward the opposite armrest, tugging at it over and over. The door is locked in its half-closed position. Mrs. Fort is leaning a bit toward the middle of the seat. "Oh my," she says, "this *is* interesting!" Her seat belt holds firm.

There is a lull now between wash and rinse and Lee looks around, desperate for a box of tissues, an old *chamois*, a dip-stick rag. Nothing.

In one continuous movement she unbuttons her blouse, wrenches her arms out of it, and stuffs it in the gaping crack over Mrs. Fort—not a second before the rinse water begins. Still, the water does not reach Mrs. Fort this time.

Now the light increases as the car moves toward the exit and the Arm of Doom descends to dry them.

Lee takes back her blouse, squeezes out the water on the

floorboard, and by the time they emerge to the swarm of boys, she is buttoning the front.

She looks at Mrs. Fort. "I'm really sorry," she says. "You okay?"

Mrs. Fort has found her purse and is patting her hair with a tissue. "Reminds me of the time I rode from here to Omaha in an open wagon. Rained around the flap all the way."

That night as they are having their coffee, Jim says, "I noticed you got the car washed today."

"Yeah," Lee says, suddenly intent on stirring. "No big deal."

"Maybe not to you," Jim says, "but it apparently was the high point in Mrs. Fort's day."

Lee looks up. "You talked to her?"

"She was out gardening when I came in."

Lee studies her coffee. "I guess she told you all about it."

"Only. . .and I quote, 'Quite exciting.'"

Lee lets the steam from her coffee fog her glasses. "Bless her," she says. "Would you believe she'd never been through a carwash?"

Lee smiles. A casual smile for Jim. A secret one for the blouse drying behind the door. A grateful one to Mrs. Fort.

III. Appearances

The Halloween Alps Boys

Lula woke and saw that a chain of blue mountains had come during the night. Saliva pooled in her cheeks when she studied their frosted tops, as white as coconut snow cones. Not even the deep orange sun could melt them. The scene was pretty, in a way, all except the hook-nosed wizard swirling up from the fender above the tailpipe. His breath was full of music aimed toward the mountains. He might give her nightmares.

She called to her stepdaughter. "Myrna, come look at this bus." Myrna was down from Milwaukee on her yearly visit to ensure her father's will had not changed and to show the neighbors that Lula was being maintained by a loving family.

Myrna came, already in her running suit. She put her hand lightly on the side of Lula's face and turned it. "Momsie, you shouldn't stand at the window in your nightgown."

"Why?" Lula formed up the word carefully. The Golden Rule: If she enunciated at others, they would enunciate back at her.

"Things show," Myrna said, still holding Lula's pale soft cheek.

No they don't, Lula wanted to say. But that was admitting she had considered the possibility. Or perhaps she could say, So? Your father was always appreciative.

It was true that her batiste nightgown revealed large brown nipples splayed against her waist, crotch hair sprigging between her legs when the light filtered through. She saw all this in the hallway mirror. As a girl, she had been required, before going out, to stand in a doorway with her legs apart, to test whether she was wearing a petticoat. Now, in her eighties, she kept behind the sheers, and never with the lamp on behind her.

Lula gestured toward the mountains. "Interesting. Blocks my view though."

She had seen the U-Haul last week, the three young men shuffling into the house with makeshift furniture. The children of her neighbor Mabel said they would not sell the house after Mabel died, but they had, and now it was a rent house. That was okay of course, because it gave her something to do, studying the comings and goings of the new neighbors.

Now visitors, yes visitors, had come in this painted bus to see the new folks. She hoped they would not stay long. "Highways or depots," she admonished them, continuing to study the bus after Myrna had brought her robe to her.

For a long time, her greatest pleasure had been looking out across the yards from her vantage at the crosspiece of the "T" the streets made. In fact, she had done it for twenty years, ever since she awakened deaf one morning. The doctors agreed that a stroke affecting both ears was rare but possible. She was fitted with the best kind of hearing aid and told to make-do.

Myrna worried Lula to death the rest of the week. Myrna's projects this visit included having dead bolts installed, getting Raul the handyman to agree to drive Lula anywhere she needed to go, and arranging for a notary to come regularly to the house for Lula to sign the insurance card certifying she was alive for another month.

Myrna's last act was to call the public works office and report the band boys to them. Hanging up, she wrote on the pad, NO MORE THAN 14 DAYS, and showed it to Lula, then said, up close to her face, "You call this number to report them if they're there after that."

Lula could dial and shout things into the phone one way. "Scum," Myrna said. "Scum is what they are. Rock band people. You be careful."

When Myrna finally took a taxi to the airport, Lula drew up her chair to the window and had an extra cup of coffee to celebrate being alone again. Cooperation was the thing with Myrna. Myrna was all

Lula had left. They had had each other ever since Bill, Myrna's father, died in his prime.

Still, one thing Myrna was right about was the bus. Apparently the bus wasn't just visiting. Lula could see nothing now, nothing of the neighborhood except those blue alps with ice on the top that never melted, not from their too orange sun nor the breath of the wizard. She agreed with Myrna wholeheartedly on the need to get rid of it, but in her own way.

Thursday at noon the boys began packing the bus. They swarmed around it, shirtless and barefoot, pushing big black boxes on rollers and winding miles of electrical cords.

Lula thought of them as boys but of course they were men, as she could readily see. If she'd had children, one might be hers right now—no, wait—her own sons would be in their fifties.

The boy with the ponytail had hair on his chest shaped like a tornado, spinning down to a little curlicue at his navel, which was well above his pants. Another had big blond tufts of underarm hair showing front and back, more evident when he was carrying something and his arms were pressed against his sides. Lula thanked God every day of her life that her eyesight was holding out.

At dusk she was trying to determine from the pictures on television what had happened that day. Peter Jennings did tiny jerks in his chair when he talked, as if certain words were ants biting him; Dan Rather had a nice head of hair like her husband Bill's up to the day he died. Then she felt in the arms of her chair that the bus had started up. She turned off the lamp and went to the window. In a few minutes, it pulled out, and she saw anew the yards that had existed only in her mind for over a week

Madge's boxwood needed a trim. Velma's black and tan clay swans had been given a "V" of chunky yellow goslings, no doubt by Velma's grown children. Beyond that, the bottle brush was beginning to bloom by Rosella's front door.

In an earlier day, these things would not have caught her by surprise. Even if there was a sudden range of mountains obstructing her view, she would have ventured out to visit the other widows.

Now they had all become so arthritic that it was both painful and dangerous to venture beyond their own drive-ways. Lula envied the others still keeping up by phone every day. Sometimes, when she thought of all the things they might be discussing, she would go to the phone, raise the receiver, and say into it, "Chat! Chat! Chat!"

It was magic the way, from the time she lost her hearing, and not long after that, her husband, she could remember everything that had gone on in these yards. She had watched a whole neighborhood of children slowly exchange riding their tricycles in circles in the driveways for throwing footballs and Frisbees in their front yards, to riding skateboards up and down the street, to mounting motorbikes, and finally, to bouncing the family cars out of the driveways and skidding off.

She saw a generation of ash trees fall in high winds, a season of grub worms destroy the lawns, periodic freezes kill everything tender. And lately, in the last few years, she had seen the houses grow quiet as first the children, then the husbands and fathers left or died and women like herself maintained their lawns with sprinkler systems and hardy shrubs and Raul the handyman.

It was Raul's kindness, to be careful not to startle her, that caused him to come shake hands with her before he began cutting her yard. He was the only man who ever came around any more on a regular basis. Most of the time she was waiting behind the door, looking through the drapes as he bent over the faucet to wash his hands first, before he pressed the button that turned on the flashing doorbell light.

Raul's hands were wide and brown, like coffee with a double spoon of creamer, and they were curiously soft to be the hands of a man who handled mowers and rakes and hoses all day. Sometimes he gently enfolded her hand in both of his, careful not to squeeze, and it was a warmth she looked forward to.

Once he brought her a bottle of rubbing alcohol into which he had stuffed some leaves. "I prepare for your *dolor*," Raul said, indicating she was to rub it well into her joints. She had done it every night for a long time, knees and hands especially, and it seemed to help. Then Myrna came, took one look at the leaves, poured it all down the sink and flipped the disposal. "Momsie, do you want to be arrested?" she asked. "Didn't you know that was marijuana?"

After that, Lula did not sleep as well because of the pain, but it was too much trouble to explain it all to Raul and get more.

At ten, Lula watched a detective show with lots of cars rolling over and blowing up, and the news, which featured mug shots of dangerous criminals. She could not hear whether they were captured or not, and so she tried to memorize their faces. She turned off the television and peeked out the drawn drapes to see if the bus had returned. It had not.

Perhaps they had taken it to where they were going to keep it permanently. She took off her hearing aid, made sure her hammer was in place on the nightstand, and taped her eyes shut with junior Band-Aids. When she told the doctor her eyes dried out at night, he said it was because her lids floated open like a baby's while she slept, and prescribed taping them shut. She hadn't wanted to at first. Myrna said do it anyway.

The next day was Friday, for many years Lula's favorite. It was the day she had her hair done in the morning and played bridge in the afternoon. But during the past year, two of the bridge foursome had died, and her driver's license had been revoked, due to a very insignificant collision. Myrna said no more driving—certainly not without a license. So she canceled her standing appointment and now all she had scheduled on Fridays was to wash her hair at the sink in the kitchen.

Today she set her hair in pin curls to dry, made a pan of lemon squares, and sat looking out the living room window all afternoon.

When the boys had not come home by dark, Lula put the lemon squares in the freezer. On Saturday, she took them out to thaw. The boy's house was quiet all day. In the evening, looking out across the lawns, she ate half of the lemon squares.

Sunday came and went and Lula wondered if the Halloween alps boys had been a mirage, a fig newton of her imagination, as she and her brothers had called it in their youth. Well, Myrna was probably right. They were no doubt scum. If they ever came back, her tactics on them would be friendly but firm. The bus had to go.

That night she dreamed she was on a lake in a canoe, with a smiling swan swimming alongside her. A motor boat came by, churning the waters, this way and that, vibrating her head with sound. Finally it zoomed off, and its wake was not ripples on the water but a slow hiss in the air. When she turned to the swan for comfort, he had the face of the wizard on the bus. It was he who was making the slow hiss.

In the dream she could hear, and that did not seem right, so she awoke to investigate. She sat up and picked the tape off one eye. She looked all around and, seeing nothing different, got out of bed and went to the window. The mountain range glowed in the moonlight. The Halloween alps boys were back.

That next afternoon Lula put on her dress with the red poppies and crossed the street with the rest of the lemon squares. The boys were awake at last.

"Hello there," she called, standing beside the curb. They were moving back and forth between house and bus, taking big strides, their long hair flopping rhythmically with their feet.

One of them looked her way. "Hi," he said, and leapt into the bus. He wore only a pair of button-up jeans. Well, at least he did not have on a jacket with strange symbols like the gangs on TV. Lula stood, waiting. Another boy came from the house. He had a ponytail and an earring that glittered in the afternoon sun. He flicked his cigarette in the bushes. She watched his mouth carefully. "What can we do for you?" he asked.

"I'm Lula Perth," she said, too loud too late. "I'm your neighbor."

"Yeah?" the boy said. "Lula, huh?" He was closer now and she could see his lips better. He did not offer his name.

Lula reached in her bosom to turn up her hearing aid. Another boy, the one with the blond underarm hair, came out of the bus now and stood too close. She could smell his sweat; it smelled like he'd been eating Mexican food.

The ponytail one said, "What'cha got there?" The other one said something that sounded like "besides tits" and they looked at each other and laughed. She withdrew her hand from her bosom. Surely he couldn't have said that.

"Lemon squares," she said, "my specialty," and with the "s" her hearing aid began to whistle. The sound was something white and Lula could tell when it began because the people she was talking to would look up suddenly like dogs catching a fresh scent.

The ponytail one reached out and took the lemon squares before she could extend them to him. It occurred to her she might never see the plate again. She tapped her bosom and the squealing sound stopped just as the boy said something.

"You'll have to forgive me," she said slowly and deliberately. "I'm hard of hearing. It's not from being old though." The boys looked at each other blankly. "It's a distinct disadvantage," she added.

There was a pause. She was going to have to ask them their names. Before she did that, though, she would try to have a little conversation. "How would you boys like it if you couldn't hear your music?"

"Bummer!" The underarm-blond boy rolled his eyes. "We wouldn't like that at all, would we, Crud?" He goosed Crud, causing Crud to juggle the lemon squares.

"Watch it, Snort!" Crud said.

"Smart?" Lula said. "Now that must be a family name. And Kurt? I used to have a beau by that name." No one said anything for a moment.

"What's your other friend's name?" She nodded toward the bus. A third boy, short and dark, had come from the house and disappeared there. She imagined he would have an ethnic name.

"Flip," Crud said.

"Philip," Lula repeated. "How regal."

Crud and Snort began backing up. Crud spoke loud. "Thanks for the cookies, Mizz—what's your name?"

"No, no rain today," she said. "I was wondering about your bus."

"What about it?" Snort said.

"Is it permanent?"

The boys looked at each other. "Man, that's how we ride," Crud answered.

"I mean, is this its parking place?" Lula asked.

Snort scratched his belly. "Home sweet home."

She took a step to go, rummaging around for the courage to quote them the city's law. "Well, enjoy my lemon squares, boys." She went carefully back over the too-long grass of their side yard.

Lula was reading about senior citizen scams in the evening paper when she first noticed the lampshade pulsing, like a little bell being rung. She sat there a while looking at it, making sure it was truly moving and not just her blood pressure acting up. She turned out the lamp and went to the window, placing her palms on the glass. The vibration traveled through her shoulders and up the sides of her neck until it made her lips tingle.

Peering into the dark, she could see the bus lit up. The lighted purple windows hovered over the mountains like a space ship. The vibrations were coming from that direction. The boys were apparently practicing their music on the bus. She held her hands a long time on the pane and licked her lips over and over. When the boys took a break, she went to bed.

The next day there was a letter from Myrna. "Has that rock band moved yet? It is entirely illegal for them to be there. Keep your doors locked, and don't forget to call the public works office."

She went immediately to the phone, lifted the receiver, and practiced: "This is Mrs. Lula Perth. I am deaf. Please do not try to talk back to me. I understand a big vehicle may not be parked longer than fourteen days in a residential section. I am reporting a vehicle in violation in my neighborhood. . ." and so on, until she got all the information out. She dialed the number and hung up, deciding she needed more practice first.

The following day she made her famous vinegar pie. It had been her Bill's favorite, and her table of bridge loved it too. The crust took a long time because the rolling pin hurt her hands. When she got the pie baked and set it to cool, she took a bath and put on her hearing aid turned up all the way. It was four in the afternoon and the boys were stirring.

Snort came to the curb this time. After he had taken the pie, she said, "Smart, could I see the inside of that beautiful bus?" She wanted to see in it before they made them get rid of it. Smart scratched his head a minute, then held his hand up signaling her to wait and dashed into the bus, she presumed to straighten up. He reappeared with Crud and Flip and they fairly lifted her up the stairs.

Their hands felt rough and strong—different from Raul's. Hands all over the place! Ooh-lah-lah! What would Myrna think? When they were all inside the bus, Flip turned some switches at a big panel and thudding began in the soles of her feet. All she could do was stand there and say, "My, oh my, boys."

The bus was not like what she had imagined. She thought there would be seats lined up in rows like on a school bus but there were, instead, loungers and a refrigerator and a big set of buttons and lights and levers mounted on one wall that could have been the NASA control room. There were purple blinds over the windows and cords and black boxes all around. The smell was of hot electrical plugs and something like an herb or incense.

When they helped her outside again, perspiration was beading on her scalp but her feet felt wonderful.

Early the next Monday Lula took sugar cookies on a paper plate and asked Snort, who came to the door rubbing his eyes, if she could have her lemon squares plate and vinegar pie pan back. He was a long time finding her dishes while she waited on the porch. When he finally brought them, they were unwashed, but that was okay.

On Thursday she got another letter from Myrna. "When you get this letter, time's up—14 days. I hope that filthy rock band has moved on. They will do nothing but devaluate the neighborhood property. Write me what you have done about them."

She sat right down at her desk: "I have called the office of public works. And, I told the boys they couldn't leave their bus there, that there was a city ordinance against such. I was firm." Then she looked in her recipe box and found her card for Coca Cola Cake.

Crud answered the door. "What'cha got this time?" he said, opening the screen and taking it from her. His odor wafted out.

"It's a Coca Cola cake," Lula said.

"Well, I'll be darned." He tasted the icing with one finger.

She strained to see behind him. All was a sour brown except for a large painting of a nude woman lying sideways, facing the front of the picture.

Now Crud was at a loss for something to say. "Y'all c'mere!" he called out behind him. Snort and Flip came forward.

"It's a Coca Cola cake," Crud said.

Snort whistled. "Look'a there!" Then directly at Lula he half-shouted, "Thanks but you shouldn't bring us all these things."

At this point she had intended to say, "By the way, I wonder if you boys would mind moving your bus to a parking lot?" but what came out was "Will you boys be having an exciting weekend?"

"Work," Snort said.

"Three days on the road," Crud added.

"I wish I could travel," Lula said. "How would you like it if you couldn't—"

They were already closing the door.

"See ya'," Flip called.

That night Lula dreamed of a man in a Panama hat beside a mountain that had arisen out of an anthill at the edge of her yard. He beckoned to her. She was terribly afraid of him and called "Myrna!" over and over but Myrna never came. Finally she unlocked her door and went out to him.

Halfway there, Lula awoke in a wave of pleasure, lingering for an instant in a perfect place, a protected sunlit place where she was totally loved. This caused something that started up from her knees and down from her chest at the same time. The feeling met in the scrunched lap of her gown.

When she had lain as long as she could in order to contain the feeling, she peeled the tape from her eyes and sat up. She dangled her feet and looked at the clock. It was 1:23. Reviewing why she was awake, she realized something had awakened her. Maybe it would repeat itself. She waited.

Soon they started—the vibrations. The bedsprings seemed to be talking in a strange language rising upward into the mattress. She spread her hands beside her and traced slow circles on the sheet, feeling the luscious waves. Something about a bed moving, even so slightly, reminded her of a thing gone forever, a thing with a man.

The man in the Panama came back, briefly this time, bringing for an instant his orange sunlight, which filled all the space between her legs.

When the feeling subsided and she thought she could stand, she reached for her glasses, and did so, pausing long enough for her hips to catch. She hobbled to the front window and looked out. The bus was lit. Shadows moved back and forth in rhythm against the purple curtains. She could see the outline of Kurt's ponytail. Of the other two, Philip was the short one. It was like a game show, by process of elimination. She pressed her hands against the pane and felt the pulsations in the glass. The feeling ran the length of her arms and spilled over into her breasts, then poured down like a waterfall, down, into her belly.

She stayed there a long time, until the windowpane stopped shivering and the lights went out in the bus. When she finally went back to her bed, she had to apply new Band-Aids to her eyes.

Lying in that extra darkness, she practiced her telephone speech: "This is Mrs. Lula Perth, a local citizen. I am deaf. Do not try to answer me back. I cannot hear you. My problem is as follows. . . ." She rearranged her aching legs and began again, "This is Mrs. Lula Perth. I am . . . ."

Then the brilliant idea struck her, literally struck her: The Halloween alps boys went out to work on the weekends. This made it necessary to start counting the days afresh each Monday morning. The bus would never be there fourteen days in a row.

Crossings

They say that astronauts' hands float when they sleep. The hands of Carlos float, touching lightly the underside of his grave, beautifully manicured hands with rings. He's finished clapping. He'd have slapped his knees if he could, bent over double, red-faced from laughter. It was a story that good, what happened when his memory crossed the Rio Grande.

One saved such stories for Tripa Club meetings, held under the stars and the mesquites on somebody's ranch, the tangled *tripas* sizzling on the grill and plenty of cold Carta Blanca.

All who knew him agree: Carlos would need a story like that to keep him entertained in eternity. For Carlos had a throttle that was wide open all the time. He was good at many things and excessive at most. *¡Impresionante! ¡Asombroso!* Bigger than life, he left it, moving off all at once, laughing and singing, in his prime.

Some deplore the circumstances, a boating accident, while others secretly admire the timing—a double-lived life, a hundred years packed into fifty. Without decline. Without forgetfulness, arthritis, or a clogged heart when the years of feasting played out their chemistry in his veins. "God deliver me from old age, " he'd roar privately when one of his elderly patients hung on to life past season. As many meals as could be a party, Carlos made them so. As many nights as could be reveled in, Carlos planned and executed. Flying in from a bank or a medical or an alumni or a philanthropic gathering, he would call home from 35,000 feet. "Go get some meat," he'd tell his wife Judy. "I want a cookout. Get fifteen pounds of fajitas and a dozen T-bones. And get a video. And call the Peñas and the Karams."

For his wife's birthday party, he had his representative claim the flag that had flown over the capitol in Austin that day and deliver it personally to her.

Once Carlos bought a ranch in the next county and then informed his family. Another time, he remembered a *marimba* band he'd heard deep in Mexico, traced them down and imported them, crossed them, for a *pachanga* in his McAllen backyard. Of course, first he had to cross a trio of workers to build a *palapa* for their stage.

Carlos loved crossings. He was one himself, born a South Texan and sent back to school in Guadalajara to learn proper Spanish. He never recognized *el rio* as anything but a piece of geography. Meeting a cousin in Sonora, a crony in Mazatlán, friends for supper in Reynosa—these were as natural to him as daylight.

In his casket, open at the back of Our Lady of Sorrows, he lay smiling, filling the whole space, full-chested, his hair still black and beautiful, his mustache commanding, his lingering presence oddly comforting—acting as both cause and effect. But for little things like breath and pulse, he would have thundered to the mourners, "Come in! Come in! So nice to see you!" folding each shaky tearful admirer in a double *abrazo*, his potpourri of cumin and garlic and beer and shaving lotion and disinfectant blending as all the incense they would ever need.

So for these and a thousand other reasons, his wife, his five children, and the general South Texas population were loath to grant Carlos his longstanding wish for a *short* happy life. Notwithstanding, she and the children determined he must have the most beautiful, the grandest monument ever to grace Roselawn.

Still, a year passes, then two. His followers—many of them his patients—continue their pilgrimage to his grave. Coordinated offerings of aqua and fuchsia, ribbons and plastic chrysanthemums, stuffed animals, notes ("Thank you, Dr. G., for saving my precious Julio," *"Gracias a Dios a Ti"*). One or two mourners confront Judy, ask where's the gravestone. "It's on order," she tells them.

Finally Judy wakes one morning with her grief intact, contained: she can act. She calls a designer. Then Mr. Gonzalez, the local monument dealer, seeing that Judy wants to order something bigger than the United States, suggests they go to Mexico, to a stone cutter up the river. They'll cross at Roma and head west. After all, death is done large and well in Mexico.

"Don't get it in Mexico," one son upstate says with an authority she is accustomed to. "You'll have too hard a time crossing it."

"Your dad never had any trouble crossing things." She has grown her own authority. And he knows to leave well enough alone.

It's a headstone but it's shaped like a sarcophagus. Carlos isn't inside but he might be, to the stranger's eye. The structure is ten feet long with a giant bivalve seashell carved in the middle like the one Botticelli's naked, wild-haired Venus steps from. In South Texas yard art, *La Virgen*—blue-clad, demure—steps from the shell. Judy smiles, wondering which woman Carlos would prefer. Neither will be on this one. Just the shell imprint on three tons of *cantera* mounted on a concrete base.

Men will haul the stone out of the Sierra Madres—God only knows how—maybe from a quarry near Horsetail Falls where Carlos went many times in his fifty packed years. He loved the mountains.

It's going to be too plain. Judy chooses blue and yellow tiles for a border.

Three months pass and Mr. Gonzalez calls. *El monumento* is ready. They must go and get it. Bring *pesos*. She meets him at the Roma crossing, parking her car and riding over with him in his pickup pulling a flatbed trailer. Outside Miguel Aleman, they pull into the stone yard.

Judy goes inside to settle up. First there's small talk, condolences, a bit of sympathetic sighing, then a deliberately complicated writing of the receipt, to justify the cost. All this takes a while and when she comes out and walks back through the broken brick and dogs and children to where Mr. Gonzalez is, the stones are already loaded. A couple of dusty workers are tying ropes over six huge mounds wrapped in—of all things—old cardboard boxes. There's lettering of orange juice and green beans and toilet paper and starch covering her husband's memory. She can't see the *cantera*, but Mr. Gonzalez seems satisfied, explaining how the sections will be fitted together.

Three tons of rock wrapped in cardboard and balanced on a flatbed trailer—it is a unique sight. They wind slowly back through Miguel Aleman and cross the small bridge, lowering to the U.S. side to idle in the line of cars. "Thank goodness the line's not long," Judy says.

"*¡Si!*" Mr. Gonzalez replies. He's a man of few words. They sit, each thinking how, if it were evening or morning, they'd be there in the middle of the bridge, the murky Rio Grande far below, doing a little math in their heads to answer whether their own weight added to the loaded trucks also in line constituted a significant architectural stress to this old pre-NAFTA structure.

When they drive into the crossing lane on the U.S. side, they are unlucky, drawing the red light that signals random inspection. The situation brings out Mr. Gonzalez. "*Aiiee*, I don't know how this is going to happen," he says mildly. An agent steps out, signaling them over. They pull into the bay, taking up two stations.

The agent leans into the window. "U.S. citizens?" They nod. "What are you carrying?"

"Rock," Mr. Gonzalez says, "for this lady's husband's monument."

"Yeah?" The agent looks back at the cardboard-covered lumps. "Well, our policy is to ask you to unload."

"Maybe I could tear one of the cardboards a little?" Mr. Gonzalez offers. "I've crossed stones before. Not this big, of course."

Judy and Mr. Gonzalez get out of the truck and stand respectfully before the United States Immigration Service. Judy is five-feet-two inches tall. Mr. Gonzalez is 65 years old; he received a pacemaker last year.

"That won't give us the whole picture," the agent says, hands on hips, one lightly on his gun.

They all stand in silence, the agent looking at the lumps, Mr. Gonzalez wiping his brow, Judy concentrating on not smiling.

Then the agent has a bright idea. "We'll bring in the dogs," he says.

It's a threat they gladly accept, to be sure—an indignity, this being sniffed by animals, but an enlightened alternative.

The agent signals the trainer and Sparkie and Tab are brought forth, happy to be released from their wire enclosures, straining toward their work.

On signal they leap to the flatbed, joyfully begin their job sniffing at the cardboard behemoths. They're confident. They check out the Joya and Pampers boxes. The trainer moves with them, calling out encouragements. They go on to Niagra and Del Monte. Once, one of the dogs returns to Pennzoil, rechecks, is satisfied. Perhaps it was only a mouse nest from the previous use of the box. Do they find drugs, contraband? It is obvious these stones have Just Said No. Humans!—what will they think up next?

But just as Carlos was irresistibly charming, so his tombstone lures and, when the dogs are called, Sparkie takes a quick break, wetting the closest lump. The trainer reddens, looks contritely at the widow Judy. "Sorry, ma'am. They're not supposed to do that."
Somewhere Carlos roars out laughing. *El que rie al ultimo, se rie mejor.* Laughing best and last, his mouthful of white teeth flashing, clapping with hands that never sleep, enjoying this joke of a little mortal drama.

And Mr. Gonzalez and the widow are excused to go their way, crossing three tons of mountain from Mexico into Texas for a mountain of a man, who crossed over *muy vigoroso* from this life into the next.

Camp Knowledge

The story was, that in the supper line, Gilbert had exposed himself to the ladies in Number 203. As he was telling them about his past as a golf pro, he had reached down, unbuckled, unbuttoned, unzipped, and, taking his own sweet time, had tucked his shirttail in. All this while quoting his scores, the tournaments he'd played in, the cups he had at home in Arizona on his mantel, the way he wished that his pretty—beautiful, really—28-year-old Uruguayan wife was with him now, but was visiting her parents for a month. Gilbert's hair was dyed red and styled in a serious comb-over.

Well, *c'est la vie*, live and let live, Cecil always said, but here was the thing: The women in 203 *said* that Gilbert exposed himself to them.

Cecil and Mildred sat facing on the double beds in their cabin. Cecil tugged off a boot and let it drop to the floor. "Mildred," he said, as though she wasn't the only one in the room at 10 p.m., "I am tired of these shenanigans."

Mildred had a round face and pale eyes. She was creaming her feet. "I don't know—"

"I do," Cecil said. "The problem is, Women have gotten to where they don't respect. First it was that snooty Dr. Nancy Prichard. How'd you feel when she took down her name sign you'd made for her on the computer and hand-colored so pretty? How'd you feel when she goes and writes her name again on the back, without the "Dr." and re-sticks it all catty-wampus on the door? I *know* she's a doctor because it's in her file on her stationery and I studied all the files last week."

Mildred frowned and inspected a corn. "I guess she—"

"And take that Jill, that dance girl, having the nerve to keep her class 'til twelve when I told her, right off, after the first day, to let them out early so they could get to the lunch line. She's doing it just to defy me."

Cecil rested his small white arms on his knees and his undershirt bloused a little. He blew down inside it to cool himself. "Now it's these ladies in 203 come with this stuff they made up. Women just love to gossip. They come reporting bunk like this and you wonder, you just wonder, what next. "

Mildred looked at him with mild astonishment. "But—but *Gilbert*, what about *Gilbert*?"

Cecil unlaced his other boot. He knew the way she thought. "Let's put it this way: Should those old maids in 203 have been noticing a man tuck his shirttail in?"

"But men don't unzip, just like that, and let their pants down in public, to tuck their shirttails in—" Mildred was as close to a challenge as she ever dared come—"do they?"

Cecil threw his boot a little distance. "I wasn't in retail sales for thirty-five years without learning a thing or two. Let me put it real plain: Women have a number of ways of requesting to see the merchandise. If they ask, there's a good prospect that they have a need for the product."

Mildred turned and tucked her feet under the covers. Her eyes rummaged the ceiling tiles searching for her husband's logic. "Are you saying those ladies were *asking* to see Gilbert's thing?"

Cecil stood and stretched, then headed for the bathroom. He loved Mildred, but at times she could be totally dense.

The camp had degenerated in two days and it was up to Cecil to turn that around pronto. Cecil and Mildred's official duties for the week long Elderlearners conference had been spelled out at the time of the interview: make room assignments; mark doors with occupants' names; help participants find meeting places; trouble-shoot, taking serious problems to the director. Cecil explained to

Mildred that these were just the minimum tasks. If he and she wanted to come back year after year for free, as camp facilitators, they'd have to prove themselves by doing more, much more.

They'd have to warn these old people—well, okay, some weren't any older than Cecil and Mildred—of the many dangers of Hill Country encampment. They'd also have to guard them, herd them, pamper them . . . "love them?" Mildred had capped off sweetly.

"Hell, no. We're not required to do that," Cecil replied. Perhaps Mildred could be a helpmeet, but Cecil figured the heavy load was on him, what with his vast experience as manager of Osgood Five-and-Dime Store.

Hadn't he whipped those salesgirls into shape, those flighty little after-school and summer-only high schoolers? He wasn't about to let a bunch of retired secretaries and housewives and uppity real estate agents get the best of him—oh yeah, and a lady doctor.

He had been a manager of a commercial enterprise, and he'd be there yet if Walmart hadn't come to town and run him out of business. Now, for his and Mildred's vacation, he was reduced to managing a camp of Elderlearners a hundred miles from home—every year if he and Mildred were lucky enough to prove their worth.

He spoke into the darkness. "Snookins, we've got twenty-nine people in our care–twenty-two women and seven men." But Mildred was mildly snoring. So he added, "It's hardly fair to have so many women over and up against the men. Anybody can see that."

The next morning Cecil went to the camp office to report the flashing incident.

The front desk girl was a lady who didn't bother to fix her hair. "Hey, Hilda," Cecil said, "I need to talk to Miz Androw." The Miz caught like a ball of cotton in his throat but that's the way she'd introduced herself on Get Acquainted Night.

"What's it about?" Hilda asked.

"It's a confidential matter," Cecil said, studying a fingernail. Just then he thought to use a term from the handbook. "Socio-dynamics of this week's group."

Hilda didn't miss a beat with her gum. "Well, Miz Androw's not here. But I'm expecting her back from town any time now. Want to leave a note?"

It was quite a walk over here to headquarters and Cecil didn't want to come back before noon. "Okay." he said. "Just give me a piece of paper and a pencil."

He went to a corner table and wrote:

Dear Ms Androw:

An incident has been brought to my attention that I feel it is best to report to you. The Elderlearner ladies in 203 have complained to me about a fellow Elderlearner they say exposed himself to them yesterday. From what they say, it looks to me like he wasn't doing anything other than tucking his shirttail in. (Whether or not they saw his privates, I did not ask—they *did* use the words "exposed" and "flashed.") I felt it was best to come to the office and report it than to have them bring charges or something against the camp.

Respectfully submitted,
Cecil Osgood, Chief Camp Facilitator

Just as he was folding the paper against Hilda's prying eyes, Miz Androw breezed in. "Hi, Cecil," she called. "Everything going okay with the Elderlearners?"

She threw her keys across the room to her desk and smoothed the waist of her shorts. Suddenly Cecil wanted nothing more than to get out. "Nearly," he said. "Actually I was just writing up an incident."

Miz Androw reached for the paper and began to read. When she finished, she burst out laughing and handed the paper to Hilda. "Read this, Hilda," she said. "Don't we wish we'd been there!"

Cecil felt his face burning. "Well," he said, "it could have been serious."

Now Hilda cackled out. She laid the paper on the counter and Miz Androw scooped it up. "You know what I think we ought to do with situations like this, Cecil?"

Before he could answer, she crumpled his note and netted a basket in the toy hoop of her waste can. "Deep-six it. Actually, Mr. Osgood, you need to learn that this sort of thing is part of what makes the Elderlearner experience so rich. You know, a little camp hanky-panky."

Cecil touched his hand to the bill of his gimme cap and backed toward the door. "S-sure thing! I get you! I'll just monitor the situation the rest of the week." A fresh batch of female laughter followed him down the porch steps.

He'd have to take another tack. Miz Androw could easily blackball him and Mildred, keep them from coming back in the years ahead. Be more careful about giving reports, and yet if something dastardly happened, it would be his fault. Nothing to do but try to keep things firmly under control.

Okay, so he was through with socio-dynamics. He'd go back to time factors, a schedule challenge. He looked at his watch, eleven-thirty, and started down the hill to The Barn where Jill was teaching Folk Dances of the World.

When he stepped in, Jill was calling out stuff on the mike but he couldn't understand a word of it. The class danced in a line, arms linked like Jackie Gleason's dancers. Jill waved to him to join them but he sat down quickly in a folding chair near the door. He had told her right off on Monday about the time factor, explained it nicely, that she'd have to let her class out ten minutes early each day so the dining hall line wouldn't have a gap in it. He had even said it in a psychology way: "Here at Camp Knowledge we all have to compromise a little for the well-being of the group, Jill."

It had not helped one bit for the dining hall supervisor to stand up later and tell the group they were welcome to come any time during the hour. A good manager could see that those stragglers from dance class interrupted the flow. But on Tuesday Jill's people were late again. Then's when he realized he'd have to ride herd on that situation until he got it straightened out.

Now Cecil sat patiently, his father's railroad watch concealed in the palm of his hand, until he could stand it no longer. They were doing those silly sidewinder maneuvers when he snapped the lid open. He would give her a little leeway before he made his move. She had the nerve to invite him to join in. But of course, how could she know that that was out of the question, what with his responsibilities?

When it was nine minutes and thirty seconds until twelve, he stood up and moved out onto the floor. Above the sound of Grecian flutes, and making a "T" with his arms, he yelled, "Time, Miss Jill. Time to let these good folks go to the hog trough."

Jill punched the stop on the tape deck. The line dancers shuffled to a halt. "Thanks, Cecil," Jill said. "We go by the wall clock." He stepped toward her, intent on making her obey, but she shouted, "Pick it up where we put it down!" And starting the music again, she caught him by the arm and spun him around so he was in the line of dancers. Dr. Prichard linked his arm, smiled her toothy smile, and they were off. "Seven step crossover!" yelled Jill, and he was propelled to the left as though his feet didn't matter at all.

When at last they stopped, everyone laughing and wiping sweat, Jill said, "Betcha' *that'll* give you a hardy appetite today! Class dismissed! And make a run for the lunch line, to help out Cecil!" She winked and cut off the mike.

Dr. Prichard turned to Cecil. He could smell her, a lilac-and-soap scent that Osgood's-Five-and-Dime had never carried. "Listen, Cecil," she said, not removing her firm, manicured grip from his arm, "you really ought to come dance with us; it's loads of fun." The swing of her silver earrings made him dizzy.

Stepping back, he slid his watch into his pocket. "Too much to do around here, Doctor. I'll let my wife enjoy the high-jinks."

Walking back up the hill alone, Cecil knew he'd lost a whole lot of respect from those people right then. Still, something was tempering his bad feelings, a vague rising of pleasure in himself. Dr. Prichard—"Nancy"—he would now call her, had lingered to speak to him. Mildred was such a dolt sometimes.

He walked faster. He had better get you-know-who under

control, slay the flesh, so to speak. "Eckcetera and eckcetera" he murmured, and went looking for Mildred.

He found her waiting for him on the stone bench near the Prayer Path. "Listen," he said, "we're going to have to eat separately today. I'll be sitting at Dr. Prichard's table, trying to get to the bottom of the charges against her."

"Charges?" Mildred said, too loud. "Charges of what?"

He gave a little yank on her elbow. "If you won't scream, I'll tell you. But come on. We don't want to be late, not after me giving the dance class what-for about it."

The official reasons were there for going to sit with her. Being a doctor and all, Dr. Prichard *might* eventually be in trouble with the law. There had been complaints lodged against her. He needed to substantiate the evidence.

First off, there was the matter of changing her identity on her door tag. Of course, it was a discourtesy to Mildred, who had personally colored the leaves and flower border with map colors. But beyond that, wasn't there some rule that if you were a doctor, you had to identify yourself at all times? The doctor's stationery said she was even a specialist, a cardiologist. And did she think she would fool anyone? What with her somber, rich-looking clothes and silver jewelry, she was a dead giveaway.

Then there was the matter of Dr. Prichard having refused to treat people for the good of mankind. One afternoon a woman had fallen down and banged her knee on a rock. Of course, they thought immediately, "There *is* a doctor in the house," and he sent a couple of the gents to her room. "Nancy" had opened her door in nothing but her bathrobe and after finding out what the trouble was, had the nerve to suggest they take the woman to the camp nurse instead.

If there was a lawsuit, maybe he would be called to testify. Now, as Cecil went over the reasons, he found his mind wandering to what color her robe was, and if the sash was tied, and what she might or might not have been wearing beneath it.

Pulling himself together, he said to Mildred, "We can't use campers like that—anti-social. Especially doctors breaking their

127

hypocritical oaths."

Now in line, Cecil noticed that some of Jill's dance class had actually beaten him and Mildred, Dr. Nancy among them. When he got his tray, he made a beeline for the doctor's table. Mildred drifted off to another group, as though she and Cecil had only met accidentally in the lunch line.

"Mind if I join you?" Cecil said, already setting his tea on the table.

And then he saw an example firsthand of what people had been saying about Dr. Nancy Prichard. While the others at the table exchanged information on their bypasses and gallbladder removals and double hernias (they kept to safe things—not colon tumors and hysterectomies—after all, it *was* a mixed table), Dr. Nancy got real interested in her soup and salad. She touched him on the arm once, requesting the salt. And when the lady on her right turned to her and said, "So what've *you* had, Dr. Nancy?" Dr. Nancy smiled like a Cheshire cat and said, "I've been real lucky." Something about the way she had smiled at him thirty minutes before made him think he might after all have genuine "rapport" with her, as the facilitator's booklet suggested. Now, he saw her give that same smile all around, and his feelings took a turn for the worse. *Everyone* had had *something* wrong with them by this time. She was lying like a dog, actually teasing them.

He finished his slaw, laid his fork down, and waited for the other women at the table to give him a little room to talk. "Dr. Nancy," he said, "from what I understand, you *have* been real lucky. But I'd be interested to know the answer to another question."

Dr. Nancy took a dainty drink of iced tea. "Okay, shoot," she replied.

He could imagine she'd learned that kind of slang in medical school. Cecil wiped his mouth with his napkin and cleared his throat. "This is something I've been wondering about for a long, long time," he said.

The good doctor seemed to twinkle at the prospect of his inquiry. "Well, wonder no longer," she said. There was that big toothy smile again. He realized for the first time that she was a little horse-faced.

"I notice from your file that you are no ordinary doctor but a specialist, a cardiologist," he said.

"You were wondering about that for a long, long time?" she said teasingly, then added, "Actually, my work was in cardiac surgery, although of course I'm retired from my practice now."

Cecil suddenly felt clever, purposely digressive. "Reminds me of a joke. Fellow asked a man what he did and the man said he practiced medicine. The fellow says, 'Heck, we all got to practice at first but when are you going to start doing it for real?'"

The campers gave little groans and kept on eating. Dr. Nancy said pleasantly, "I've heard that one many times."

Cecil took a bite of green beans and chewed. "But back to what I wanted to ask you."

Dr. Nancy reached for her custard. "I'm ready." Her thin silver bracelets jangled.

"Don't you think there are some occupations that either a man, or a woman, can do better than the other?"

"No," she said quickly, her face going cold and blank. "I think a man or a woman can do just about anything they have a gift for and make up their minds to do."

He tried again. "You're the exception, of course, but don't you think there might be some specialties, like heart and cancer, that there's just too much at stake for a woman—a smart woman good at a million other things, you understand—to handle?"

He felt the attention of the other women at the table. They were probably glad he had brought this out in the open. "For example, when you were 'practicing,' didn't you ever have somebody tell you that you couldn't operate on them because you were a woman?"

Dr. Nancy stopped eating her custard and looked over the top of her glasses. "I never did," she said evenly.

Cecil surveyed the table. Everyone was listening. "Not anything against you being a woman, of course, but if I was to come to you and your shingle just said "M.D." and then you said you wanted to cut on my heart, I'd have to think about it a while."

"So would I," Dr. Nancy said, clicking her spoon on the fluted custard bowl.

Then she added, "Maybe I'd 'practice' on your prostate first."

There were gasps and titters, and one abruptly rose and hauled off her tray. Cecil felt his bald forehead tingle with the rush of blood and then he heard his mind's voice saying Ooh-la-la.

Dr. Nancy laughed easily. There was her hand again lightly on his arm. "Just kidding," she said prettily, and he noticed for the first time her shell pink fingernail polish. Maybe she had spoken like that to throw the others off-scent.

Later, when Mildred asked Cecil about his fact-finding mission, he said, "Oh, *that*. She's in the clear."

The Thursday night talent show lasted far longer than anyone wanted it to. A husband-and-wife piano duo played and played. Then a preacher told a dozen jokes, and the oldest woman there declaimed several original poems. Gilbert, dressed in *lederhosen* and a feathered cap, insisted on dancing a dance he said had been in his Bavarian ancestors' family for 500 years.

One more day and the camp would be over. Cecil was relieved. They'd had a vacation like other people. He'd tried his best to keep things under control. Mildred had kept her fool mouth shut (about all he could expect besides her coloring the door signs). Maybe, with a little luck, they'd be asked back next year.

After the talent show, they were moseying leisurely back to the cabins, in two's and three's, when a woman in front let out a hollow whoop. Cecil reached for Level 3 power on his flashlight, stumbled over a root, and charged the group. "Coming through. Facilitator coming through."

A wide circle of campers had spilled down below the walkway. Between two doors of the cabins, its head ranging back and forth testing the air, lay a large dark snake.

The single women clutched each other, their handbags dangling randomly. The few men had taken firm hold of their women's arms. "My God," said a woman wishing to lay claim to the discovery. "It made me pee in my pants when I first saw it. To think, it was right in front of my cabin door."

"Do something, Cecil!" shouted another.

Cecil cast his flashlight directly at the snake's eyes. He would blind it. That's what he would do.

"Everybody back!" he yelled, and waved his free hand in a swatting motion.

"We *are* back!" one called, for by now they had retreated to the grape arbor below the cabins.

"Anybody got a gun?" a man shouted.

"That's against the rules," several countered.

Gilbert spoke next. "We used to stomp 'em to death when I was in Panama." He looked down past his white legs to his dingy tennis shoes. "It'd be easy if I had on my field boots."

Cecil tried to summon up words from his old scout manual. Did you run away from them, or did you confront them by waving your arms and shouting? If this thing wasn't directly in front of the doors, he'd order everyone to their quarters.

Then an idea occurred to him. He backed a few steps to the end of the walkway, and rushing inside his and Mildred's cabin, grabbed a towel. Out again, he called, "Stand back. Stand clear, please. I'm in charge. I'll take care of this."

He edged forward, approaching the snake from the side, moving with his back against the wall, his stomach protruding each time he slithered across a doorknob.

Quite close now, he bided his time, and when the snake ranged in another direction, Cecil darted in and dropped the towel squarely over the loose form.

The snake, knowing a towel attack for what it was, scooted from under the snowy object and went on his way into the night.

Cecil sucked in his first good gulp of air in five minutes. He drew himself up to full height. "Folks, always remember that we are in the wild," he said. "Never, but never come this way without your flashlights fully engaged. We've had a close call. I'll be writing up a report on this tomorrow."

"No need," said a voice from out of the darkness. It was Dr.

Nancy. "That was an indigo," she said, "and they're on the endangered list. This is their northernmost territory. They're non-venomous—actually beneficial since they eat rattlesnakes." She came up from the grape arbor and smiled at Cecil. "Next time, besides joining our dance group, you really must take the nature course."

Later that night, when he and Mildred had gone to bed, Cecil lay a long time in the dark staring up at the ceiling tiles illuminated by the moon. They were etched with mildew clouds from an old rain leak. Mildred had gone to sleep almost immediately.

That was the way it would always be, him on sentinel for the world. Awake when others had let down.

Cecil raised the sheet and looked all the way to his toes, studying carefully in the moonlight his pajama-clad facilitating self. He checked his fly. There was no motion, even when he assigned Dr. Nancy's soft pink fingernails to the snaps.

He lowered the sheet and tucked himself in like a model hospital patient. He had done his best all week, but word would surely get back to Miz Androw about the snake. One of these clacking biddies would tell her how he dropped a towel over it, a harmless, even beneficial snake, and he'd hear Miz Androw and Hilda guffawing all the way from headquarters.

His life in retirement had started out clear. Now it was a blur. A light pain welled in his left biceps and he welcomed it if it was a heart attack, for he wouldn't have to be in charge of his and Mildred's life anymore. And if so, would Dr. Nancy rouse herself and minister to him? He wouldn't let that selfish dame touch him! But would she come? And would she rest fingers with pink nail polish on his pulse?

Osgood's-Five-and-Dime had been a sure thing. You ordered a gross of handkerchiefs, you got a gross of handkerchiefs. If instead you got a gross of dishrags or dust cloths, you sent back the mistake.

He had been under the impression that life after the store could be managed as certain. But it wasn't going to be like that. No tally balanced to the penny at end of day between the cash drawer and the register tape.

Life now was fuzzy, like the edges of Mildred's snoring, which he was helpless to change. Life now was full of puzzles, like a "good" snake that wasn't to be touched, that could crawl, scot-free, off into the dark.

Wheels

The Pentagon is not exactly a wheel. Don smiles a lopsided smile when he thinks of his former workplace thumping along on its five sides in the great scheme of things. Still it's part of the circular objects that have figured in his life.

Don is out in the garage on his new electric three-wheel cart. He told his neighbor, the father of the groom, that he'd be slower than a snail going backwards without it, that he wouldn't take anything for it. He got it the same week Doc told him to think twice before he drove his vintage '69 Northern Blue Ford Mustang convertible anymore.

So when he got his cart, he felt his life circling back again, a little more like an R&R canceled than some hocus-pocus reincarnation. The two vehicles definitely were not an even trade. He drives his cart hell bent for leather in any hallway that's longer than the one from the bedroom to the bath. That might be the parish hall, city hall, or concert hall. Don is moving on, be damned his Parkinson's.

Now Don is running a dry mop over the mag wheel spokes. Magnum 500, to be exact. Though they came with the car, they cost too much to be sitting here flat-siding in the garage. That's what got him to thinking about the Pentagon: these wheels would look like the Pentagon after a while.

When he retired and bought the Mustang, his plan was to have it out on the road at least once a day, blinding people alongside the freeway. Blow out that 4-barrel carburetor regularly. Stretch that 302 engine. Joy riding 2800 pounds of pure pleasure and not a bit

135

ashamed of it. The wind shaving his head on both sides like a fresh recruit's. Hell, not everybody got to be James Dean when he was young.

He never dreamed he'd be doing what he's doing today. Back then, he wouldn't anymore have loaned out his Mustang to anybody, much less his kids or somebody else's, than he would have gone AWOL fifteen years into career military service.

So for a while, he did take the Mustang out once a day—or night (sometimes he wanted to go at night just to use the four head-lights), until his accelerator foot went AWOL. Always before, when he said, "I'm giving you a command," it would say, "Yes, Sir," and take him and that Mustang where he told it to. Now it was often surly, recalcitrant.

Still, he likes to sit in the driver's seat and now he opens the door and, after several tries, transfers himself into the deep blue vinyl. With some coaxing, his long legs follow. The interior always shocks him with pleasure, though he doesn't think of it like that.

Only this time the effort has made him dizzy. He bangs his head against the back of the bucket seat (a major improvement, in his estimation, over the original ones still in there when he bought it from a bankrupted Mustang fancier). Now the dash comes clear before his eyes, like a couple of amphitheaters side by side where a drama will be played out. His special-ordered wooden steering wheel feels cool to his hands.

Don keeps a polishing rag on the seat and he leans over and touches up the glove compartment catch, a little silver Mustang running in the wind, all four feet off the ground. He exercises his mind with remembering all the locations on the car for attaching one of these ponies: hood—of course, trunk catch, dome light, front fender. . .he plans to get that front fender one next, even though it's got "302" on it and that actually came in on the '68 models. He had to be right in the military, the whole nine yards or not at all. He'll do damned well what he pleases now.

The thought of these sleek animals running all over his classy muscle car inundates him, and his eyes fill with tears. He sucks in his breath and a little sob passes his lips. When he first began these crying spells, he refused to believe the tears were his, ordered them to cease and desist. But now he's grown used to all the dumb stuff that traipses through his brain. He was bitter for a while at this excess—great waves of chemicals dumping in his skull and over-running his eyes, when what he needed was this same surge charging his muscles.

He focuses on polishing the rear-view mirror. When he gets this baby back after the honeymoon, he's ordering color-keyed dual racing mirrors. Installing them himself. He checks the floor mats, stamped with Mustang. They are centered. Like dress inspection. Things have to be right.

He'd better get out while he can, before he stiffens up and has to blow the horn for his wife to come and help him back to his cart. It's not one of his better days. He takes one leg out. While he's waiting for the other one to cooperate, an instant dream comes to him, as it often does these days.

He's back at the Pentagon, dressed in his Army uniform, his shirt front holding the ribbons of his medals. There's the red and blue of his Bronze Stars, the pink of the Legion of Merit, the green and yellow of his Commendations. There are others—orange and red and green, but he'd have to look them up in his manual now to remember what was what.

He's handling BOM's—blue office memos. He loves to see people's faces when he says, "I handled BOM's at the Pentagon during the Cold War." The rule on the BOM was to say everything on one page, even if it was about an entire classification of missile, even if it was a multi-million dollar contract. In the dream, his assignment is to get his whole life on one page, on one BOM.

He'd do it with wheels. First, the huge circular saw blades of the lumber mills in North Carolina ripping up the lumber for his father and brother and cousins all around, steely rotating jaws he walked away from forever when he got the scholarship to West Point.

Then all the post assignments, the tires purchased from the PX, the spokes of trips out and back to his wife and children, the meaningless circular instructions of superiors, the compasses circling war zones on maps, the drumming of the rotor on the LOACH over him night after night in Viet Nam.

While he watches it with interest, his other leg lifts and moves his foot sideways, over the threshold of the car. Back on his cart, he takes several deep breaths and blows out through his mouth. It is a way to get rested.

He motors over to his workbench and taking up an old sheet his wife has donated to the cause, begins to tear long strips from it. When he has torn several, he looks at what's left. It will do; it's about trunk size. Angling back and forth, he maneuvers his chair alongside the workbench and spreads out the remnant of sheet, then lurches up and grips the side of the bench. He flounders, thinks he'll probably go down on the cement—it won't be the first time—then miraculously steadies.

Braced on one arm, leaning his upper body over the bench, with a precision that sometimes comes on him suddenly, he prints "Just Married" with a black marker, going over and over the letters until they're brazen and fat. He falls back into his chair and wipes the sweat from his face with a small leftover of sheet.

After a little while, he finds some thin rope and attaches a segment to each corner of the sign. The tying reminds him of staking tents and a vague uneasiness enfolds him. . .a time they were ambushed in a make-shift camp. He grimaces, checks the dark wave of fear rising in his heart, slings his head to dispel the streaks of fire coming out of the jungle.

When he's finished, the knots are snug, all even, all the same size. Now he wheels first to one side of the Mustang and then the other to attach the sign across the trunk. After a long while, the sign is centered, neat and secure.

He must rest. He takes his cart out into the driveway, down to the shade of an elm. It surprises him how good the sign looks. "'At'll hold 'em," he murmurs. By God, they better not spray paint his Mustang or fill it with shaving cream.

His head drops to his chest. In the twilight of a catnap he's just been promoted to full colonel. The groomsmen march by in parade, saluting him in the reviewing stand. In the last rank, alone, marches the groom. When he's almost out of sight, he reaches in his pocket, turns, and waggles the keys to the Mustang. The weight of Don's new insignia is monumental. He can hardly stand up.

Don jerks awake, wipes a little pool of spit from the corner of his mouth and squeezes the accelerator on the handle of his cart. Back in the garage, he removes a bottle opener from a drawer, rolls to the recycling bin and begins punching holes in the bottoms of aluminum cans. When he has a lapful of cans, he threads them on the strips of sheeting, knotting after each can. Just for the hell of it, he tests his strength by trying to crumple a can. His right hand fails the test. "Ha!" he says to his left hand when it succeeds.

Wheeling to the rear of the Mustang, he attaches the sheeting with the cans to the bumper. They look great. He goes into the house to tell his wife he's finished. Got to shower, got to sleep.

The groom, Don's neighbor's boy, is tall. His bride is beautiful. When they roll away from the church, her veil lifts, flares out so she must grab at the headpiece to keep it on her head. To Don, seated on his electric cart by the neat clipped hedge at the entrance to the church, it looks for all the world like his Mustang has taken wings, an improbable giant blue beetle rising on gossamer.

He feels the tide of tears starting far out in his private sea, the undercurrent mounting speed just below the surface, widening as it presses for shore, about to inundate him, his tuxedo, the wedding guests. It is a happiness he never felt giving commands, writing BOM's, ordering in fire power.

Just as his tears break—the white foam on the crest of the wave like the Mustang's wings, like the girl's veil—he throws his face upward and adds a loud "Hooooooooooo!" to the catcalls and whistling of the other guests. With his good left hand he feels for the red horn button on the panel of this present set of wheels.

This is not the Mustang. But some place near the center of a circle of new joy, Don honks his cart horn over and over and over.

Ruling Passions

"Save me, O Jerusalem!" Augusta Baines Collier murmurs when she sees the roach grazing on Prim's cat chow. The insect moves like a tiny orchestra conductor, his wings a frock coat, his antennae beating time to a silent concerto. Augie is absolutely sure that Mr. Collier's ghost is making a mockery of her, causing her to see in her beautiful music and poetry, insects nasty and damnable. She will be strong. She will restore her life to art.

Augie is already dressed in her town shoes but she unlaces one black oxford and hurls it at the roach. "Get! Get, Mr. Collier!" Let him come as he may—she will name his ghost for what it is. The shoe upsets the bowl; the roach evaporates.

She lays her head, replete with gray curls, on the table and weeps real tears. After a while, she rolls her head to one side and speaks. "What! Shall I ever sigh and pine?" Now that Mr. Collier is dead, she has been indulging herself. Last night she read from her George Herbert volume.

Augie goes over the facts: Mr. Collier and she were married for ten too-long years. Mr. Collier has been dead six weeks. She cannot remember why she married him, only that it was a porch swing decision long after she had dedicated her life to poetry and the organ. She certainly never realized that with the addition of "Collier" to "Augusta Baines" on the church bulletin, the smart-alecky youngsters in the church would start calling her the ABC lady.

But she takes responsibility for the bad decisions of her life, as well as the good ones. She read this in a magazine.

To provide her a decent home. To appreciate her artistic nature. To keep bugs out of her life. These were the things she asked of Mr. Collier. He provided the decent home.

And although he allowed her to keep her job as church organist (because, of course, there was a salary involved), he broke her heart when he refused to understand her poetry.

One evening when they were first married, Augie trusted him with her collection of poems, poems full of powerful metaphors such as "My organ is God laughing and crying," and lovely rhymes:

> My chrysanthemum bulb
> Against the earth doth rub.

After an hour of her recitation, the brute said, "They sound nice, but you could say things plainer."

As for keeping bugs out of her life (a small favor in return for providing a man clean clothes and wholesome meals), one might say Mr. Collier had abused her with his stubbornness and negligence. She had asked him, at first sweetly and playfully, to be her protector —not from dragons, merely dragonflies. Mr. Collier had laughed at her serious heart palpitations when a roach flew into her face as she opened her music cabinet. He would not get up at night to kill the moth fluttering behind the shade (Oh, she had had many a sleepless night listening to that bat!-bat!-bat! against the pane. What a way to commit suicide—to flutter yourself to death!)

Mr. Collier had canceled her monthly standing appointment with the exterminator. As a result, silverfish gnawed so at her *Etudes* that now, right in the middle of an offertory, a page might crumble as she started to turn it. He refused even to rejoice with her over the seventeen gnats she had trapped in a bowl filled with dissolved Efferdent and placed surreptitiously among her African violets.

The last straw was summer times. One year the cicadas sang so loud in the mesquites outside her windows she begged him to take her away to Colorado, give her nerves a little rest. He said he admired their song, "admired" his exact word.

Finally, she was forced to pray for deliverance from his ridicule and neglect. Soon after, she got relief: Mr. C died one bright morning while picking his teeth.

Now Augie stands, blows her nose on a tissue from the cuff of her dress sleeve, retrieves her shoe, rights Prim's chow. She finds her music, her car keys, her purse. Regardless of how shaken, she will go to the church to practice Sunday's music. She will get out of this bug-ridden ghost house. She will be positive. Remembering that the organ man has been in town this week for her organ's annual check-up, she affirms, "Life is good." She read this in a magazine.

In the car, driving toward town, she reflects on how the bugs have increased—like the plague on the Egyptians—since Mr. Collier's death. The morning after the funeral, black inchworms appeared on the carpet, like *tenuto* markings over notes to be held out firmly. Some curled suddenly into F clefs on the couch; some writhed on their backs in trill signs on the bathroom tiles. She pinched them up in toilet paper, flushing after each capture. New ones appeared every morning for a week. They were the first of many bugs to infiltrate her musical depths, to let her know the extent of the dead Mr. Collier's malevolence toward her sensitive nature.

The next time she noticed the persecution was when tiny sugar ants filed over the windowsill into the kitchen. Waiting for her coffee to brew, she thought she saw the dotted line after the *octavo* sign telling her to take it up or down an octave. The ants had already *crescendoed* to the sugar canister, mobilized to thirty-second notes on the way to the cupboard, and taken down her fig newtons a whole octave. She flung the package into the backyard and soaked the windowsill with spray.

After the inchworms and ants, she lost track of the order Mr. Collier used to insectify her music. There were pillbugs, rollie-pollies rocking in corner cobwebs like nervous Mozartian eighth notes. There were wasps racing about in *presto tempi* near their nest by her back door. Once, a mite of some sort came unbidden out of nowhere to bite her, *staccato* style, all over her abdomen while she slept.

And then Mr. Collier went on to attempt the ruination of her poetry. One day her eye was snared by, charmed, taken with, a beautiful word—"Trilobite"—on the spine of a book at the library. She felt she had been put under a spell and *led* to look at it. The word had that "trill" feeling and simply "tripped" off her tongue and she thought she might rhyme it with "acolyte," so she copied it into her poem notebook. But later, when she looked it up, it turned out to be a 570-million-year-old ancestor of the roach. So there she was, having been misled by Mr. C's ghost, left with only an eraser smudge where she could have had the beginning of a new poem.

When Augie arrives at the church, she takes a while letting herself in. She loves this part, the cool, dark silent chancel, the sudden flood of lights on the console when she flips the switch, the sound of rolling back the keyboard cover to reveal the manuals. First today is the Widor "Fantasia" with that wild independent pedal melody. She fishes her soft black special-ordered pumps from the bench and ties them on.

It is not until she studies the settings on the first page of her music and, repeating them aloud, pops the stops left and right, that one hand comes to rest on the piece of paper. It is a small green note propped between "E" and "G" of the middle octave on the "Swell" manual. Her heart quickens—maybe someone has left her a poem:

> A cricket apparently
> alive and well inside
> the 8 ft. principal
> (Great, C #8)—thus
> difficult to tune.
> Probably more to come.
> Sorry.
> —James Nelgin, tuner

Mrs. Augusta Baines Collier puts the note squarely on top of the Widor "Fantasia." With her right foot she tilts the crescendo pedal to top volume. She leans forward and begins to play the middle manual with her forehead. Her right fist pounds the treble, her left the bass. In a moment, she drops her full weight to the foot pedals and the *fortississimo* causes the church secretary down the hall to pause a moment listening for thunder.

The great tide of sound travels out the roof, off into the skies on the backs of a vast group of startled pigeons, notifying God that Mrs. Augusta Baines Collier intends to be her own mighty fortress against the bugs of this world.

The Day I Went To Visit My Innards

I never intended to make an appointment with my innards. You might have to make a date with your girl or the dentist but not with your innards.

But then again, I never intended to have some of them out. About a year before, I woke up one morning north of Albuquerque and passed a bunch of blood. When I saw it, I said flat out loud, "You've got cancer. You've gone and taken up with cancer."

Well, I just pulled on my pants, went out to my rig, made my delivery, then let the throttle out all the way back to Texas.

I don't know what I thought crossing the state line would do for me. My mind was batting around like one of those bingo number-picking things that blows a bunch of ping-pong balls around in a little cage. I guess I was hoping my lucky number would land in the little cup and that blood back there could be a secret between me and New Mexico.

Still, when I got back to Borger, I told Sue about it and she threw a fit so I told myself I'd see about it to satisfy her.

Dr. Winkel's been our doctor since before the beginning of the age. His office is at the corner of Main and Juniper. I've often wondered what a family does when their doctor gets old and dies. Funny, but it seems kind of disloyal of the doctor. I mean, he goes and does the very thing he's been fightin' against all these years. Well—but why am I talking like that? Of course, Dr. Winkel wasn't dead when I went to see him.

147

I wouldn't say he and I were good friends, but we had a kind of tie, and that was hunting in the fall with the same group of men on the same deer lease. Some years, that's the only time I'd see him. Other years, I'd see him quite a bit, because he doctored Donald Joe and Jeanie Sue when they were little. For that matter I knew Dr. Winkel's nurse, Mari, about as well as I knew Dr. Winkel—though it goes without saying that I'd never gone hunting with her. But Mari is a real sweet woman. She was just as nice as could be when Sue had the kids, and then she was nice to them when we'd take them in over the years with runny noses and for their school shots and so forth.

The night before I went in to see the doctor, my stomach hurt like crazy. I kept getting up all night to go to the bathroom until finally the cockroaches didn't even seem to mind me turning on the bathroom light. They went on about their business right there around my feet. Whatever their business is. I'd never seen one doing anything productive. At least ants carry crumbs and mosquitoes bite you.

Finally, there wasn't any use making the run back to bed, so I sat there and counted the tiles on the floor and wondered who Sue would marry after I died in about a year, and whether Donald Joe and Jeanie Sue would get to go to college if they wanted to.

Even though I knew better, I dreaded that appointment like I dreaded a haul to Houston. Once I got lost in Houston, and it was 24 hours before I found the warehouse. At least I was going to a familiar place.

But when I got there, I saw Dr. Winkel had bought new flowered furniture for his waiting room, taken in a new man, added another nurse, and put up a little glass cubicle with a woman inside at a computer. You can't believe how it unnerved me.

Sure enough, the new nurse, a little slip of a thing, came to get me. Kathi—I got that from her name tag—said, "Right this way," and then is when I realized Dr. Winkel had remodeled throughout—with a low ceiling, more exam rooms, lots of indirect blue lights, and a carpet. I wanted to bolt. If I hadn't felt so bad I would have bobtailed it out of there.

Kathi weighed me and took my temperature and asked me why I was there.

I didn't want to hurt her feelings, but I wasn't about to tell her anything. So I said, "I'm just here for a check-up. Kinda tired lately. When you get to be 45 years old, you'll understand."

She smiled and rested her pen on the chart. "It says here 'rectal bleeding.' You must have talked to Dr. Winkel over the phone."

My stomach hadn't been feeling too good and it'd been well over an hour since I left the house, so when she caught me in that lie, it *really* knotted up and I thought I was going to have to excuse myself.

Instead, I crossed my legs fast as a jack-knife and laughed—kind of a careful laugh though. "Oh yeah. I did mention that to him."

Kathi got ready to write again. "Okay. When was your last bowel movement?"

I was beginning to understand the lay of the land. I knew perfectly well it had been about an hour, but I studied how to say it. Seems like to say, "One hour and fifteen minutes ago" was showing you were paying too much attention to that sort of thing. So I said, "This morning." Kathi made a notation.

"What was the consistency?" I felt like I was on a quiz show going for broke. I hadn't ever described to another person what I did in the bathroom, much less to a nineteen-year-old girl named Kathi. Now that I think about it, her not having an "e" on the end of her name kind of unnerved me.

I searched around for a word. "Loose." I know I colored.

Kathi wrote. "Did it have blood in it?"

"Yep."

"Was it a black tarry substance or bright red?"

"Pretty red," I said.

She stopped writing and looked straight at me. "Was it a little or a lot?"

I felt something inside my head crack open. I think I even heard it. It was the sound of a turtle or armadillo shell when it's hit out on the road. "You mean the blood or the whole thing?"

"I'm sorry," Kathi said, "the blood."

I was hurting real bad by that time. "Beats me. Hell, I don't know what's a little and what's a lot."

She looked full of disappointment that I wasn't helping her more. "Maybe like a teaspoon, or like a half a cup?"

I had to admire that little gal. She was bound and determined to do her job. I sighed and shifted around on the stool. "All told, it must of been a half a cup."

"What do you mean by 'all told'?"

In my head, the armadillo was just lying there on the road, guts strung out, the echo of that crunch going on and on like in a shooting gallery.

I looked straight at her. "I mean I was on the toilet the better part of the night and I guess I lost that much all told."

"I see," Kathi said, and wrote some more on the chart.

When Dr. Winkel came in, I noticed he had grayed more in the months since I'd seen him. We talked a little about the deer lease and whether the season was going to be any good or not. Then I told him all in one breath about the blood in Albuquerque and high-tailing it home. I hadn't really spelled it out over the phone. I even beat him to the draw and told him I knew it couldn't be much else but cancer and how long did I have.

He said, "Not so fast, Bill. We're going to take this thing slow. I'll order some tests, we'll look at the results, and if it's the big C, we'll get you the best help we can find." He wrote a little more and handed me some papers. "Bill,"—he looked at me in that I'm-telling-you-the-gospel-truth way—"the next few days you'll feel like you was on the business end of a Roto-rooter."

He slapped the chart shut and started for the door, then said over his shoulder, "We'll talk some more later about huntin' this year, okay?"

I've already told you more about my guts than I first intended to, so I'll skip over the next few weeks by just saying that I got so used to dropping my drawers and having people run tubes and lights in me that after a while, it seemed like these things had been happening to me all my life. And that there was a big industry in this sort of thing, generally hidden and secret from the public, but at least as big as IBM or Ford when you got onto it and found yourself a customer or stockholder or whatever.

Then you started meeting the same people over and over again. First in the drugstore the evening before the tests, buying their Fleets and that awful yellow liquid dynamite that would blow you out of bed at 4 a.m.

And lo and behold, when Dr. Winkel sent me over to Big D, there they were up in Dallas again at the Medical Complex. We looked like a bunch of pervert choir members standing around in the doorways of the x-ray station in our short white gowns. I never got one of those little cup-towely things that had a decent tie or snap on it and it looked like neither did anyone else, so we spent the whole time clutching at our behinds to keep from exposing ourselves.

We made up our own little games to keep ourselves from dying of shame on the spot. The object was to tell how your body had let you down worse than all the rest.

"Fell unconscious in the bathroom and lay that way four hours until my son happened by. . . ."

"A wonder you hadn't died, but listen, I lost a quart of blood inside of an hour. . . ."

"But you're here to tell about it. I know I had this friend. . ."

And then's when we started on the second generation stories.

The long and the short of it, and believe me, there was more long than short by the time I got through, was that I didn't have cancer, but I did have something else I'd never heard of —CUC—and wished to God I never had. Seems I'd had it for a long time. Some people were sick for years with Chronic Ulcerative Colitis, and some, like me, just showed up with it after it had done its dirty work and ruined their colons.

The trouble with CUC, besides having to quit your job, losing weight, sitting on the throne day and night, having constant fever and pain—the trouble was two things: you couldn't get any sympathy from people because you couldn't spell out the details, and eventually, you had to have an operation and have it all taken out or you'd get cancer.

That's how I wound up at the Medical Complex making an appointment to visit my innards.

"Will Friday at 4 p.m. be all right with you?" the lady beside my bed asked. At these big hospitals they have people that are like USO directors. They go from room to room asking sick people if they think they can possibly squeeze in time for physical therapy on Thursday morning or a sugar diabetes study first thing next Monday, or in my case, a trip to the pathology lab.

"I had planned to go dancing that afternoon but I guess I could call it off," I said.

She grinned. "An aide will take you down in a wheelchair; I'll set it up." She patted my arm and was gone.

When I started all this, I liked to never got the hang of staying alive in a hospital. The things they do to you in a hospital—well, you think at the time you'd just rather go ahead and die than endure them. You have to give up, give up completely, just pull her over alongside the road and take the keys out of the ignition and say, "I quit." Many's the time I felt so bad, all that saved me was knowing my pants and boots were in the closet, the real me waiting in there in the dark, my belt buckled up, a bill of lading in my hand.

Now I don't want you to get the idea I'm some kind of prig. Truckers' stop johns are not for the faint of heart. And I've told, and listened to, my share of doctor and nurse jokes. But let me tell you, you hit that hard white bed and they start coming at you with all those rotten things they do, well, it's not funny like those dirty jokes and sex gizmos.

After a while, giving up felt good. Maybe I went a little over-board asking to see my colon. But after all, people took their gall-stones home in a little bottle. My sister's appendix sat pickled on the shelf over her bed for five years.

I readjusted the tubes hanging out of me and took a peek at the 13-inch scar going down my middle. It took a little detour around my navel so that the whole thing wound up looking like a giant question mark. The bag with the "efflux" (they have a nice clean name for everything nasty) lay on my right side like a forgotten water balloon.

Sue had gone back to Borger to be with the kids, and it was just as well. She was a pretty unflappable girl, but I didn't know if she'd think I had cracked up for wanting to see my colon.

I hadn't told anyone else after I told my friend Tom. "It's something I have to do. I want to make sure it was bad," I explained. "I wake up nights wondering. Just sit up and sweat about it. At the time, I was hurting so much I didn't care. Now I think if I could have held out a little longer. . .some people get over this thing. Maybe I traded my birthright for a mess of pottage, you know."

I saw Tom's hand go to his throat and then he pretended to scratch a mosquito bite. "Yeah." He looked across my bed and out the window. "Do you think the Cowboys are ever gonna' get it together again?"

Friday afternoon dragged by. I got up a couple of times to watch the Med-vac helicopter taking off from its pad. It made me want to get back behind the wheel of my rig and see that flashing center stripe again. I wondered if I'd ever have the balls to haul cross country again. I stood straight and the new scar pitched a fit.

"Mr. Watkins, you ready?" Joe stood in the doorway. "I understand you've got a 'pointment with pathology." There was a little tease in his voice.

Joe was huge and he and I had been through a lot together. I know it didn't mean a thing to him, but I was beginning to feel he and I had been lifelong buddies. We got the damned ostomy bag emptied and cleaned and then he helped me in the chair and started on the tubes. He changed the IV over so that the little bags were swinging on a pole attached to the chair. He emptied the catheter bag—thank God—and hung it on a hook on the side of the chair. He put little temporary doo-dad stoppers on the two drain tubes coming out of my sides and pinned them to my gown. Then he put a temporary clamp on the tube coming out of my nose.

He laughed softly. "Don't you look fine, Mr Watkins!" Right at that time, Joe was the only person on earth that could get away with saying that to me. Oh, my friends had said other things when they

153

called or came to visit. Some said they sure were glad everything had come out all right, or that I'd got this behind me. I'd think about those expressions and laugh my head off when they were gone.

One of my trucking buddies came over here and told me I sure had a lot of guts, going under the knife. He colored real deep after he said it. The one I liked the best was when somebody asked me what my gut reaction was to something. I couldn't help it. I said, "Hell, I don't have one of those anymore."

We started out. Once, going down a long hall, I thought of telling Joe I'd changed my mind. To take me back. I felt like Aunt Bertie who lived across the street from the funeral parlor and made herself unpopular by regularly visiting the lying-in-state room so she could tell the family of strangers how "natural" their loved one looked. But it was too late to back out. Besides, I'd never know whether I'd made the right decision or not. For that matter, I might look at it and still not know.

We stopped at a door that said "Pathology Consulting." Joe wheeled me through. It was a small room with a low counter. Joe went around to a phone, punched a button, and said, "Mr. Watkins, four o'clock, is here to see his specimen."

In a minute a door bumped open and a man in surgical greens, complete to the mask, came out carrying what looked like a turkey roaster pan covered with a napkin. Now this took me completely by surprise. I had been prepared for a snake-looking thing sloshing around in a big pickle jar but not a piece of meat in a turkey roaster.

The man behind the mask set the pan on the counter in front of me. He told me his name—it was a foreign one—and that he was chief of pathology. Then he took the napkin off. I didn't know whether to say hello or spit on it. It was gray, about three feet long, and one big mess—but then, what did I know? It wasn't like link sausage, like the encyclopedia pictures. It wasn't all gleaming pink and red either. I tell you what it looked like, and excuse me if this is—was—your favorite barbecue cut, but it looked like the world's biggest fajita.

"Vee cut it laterally for zee examination," Dr. Gorba-somebody said, moving it around with some ice tongs. "And it has shrunk considerably."

"Show me the bad part and then show me a good place." I wanted to make the comparison with my own eyes and know for all time that it'd been necessary.

Dr. G. looked at it for a moment, then said, "Oh, zat von't be possible. It simply von't be possible."

So. They didn't know after all. They just guessed. I was madder than hops. I sat there a minute clutching the armrests. Finally I thought to say, "Why not?"

"Because zere are no good places to show you. It was totally diseased—one of zee verst ve've ever received." He bent over the pan and pointed. "See all zeeze little ripples? That is zee disease."

I strained to see what he saw. The little ripples looked like the tenderizer had gone berserk on the fajita.

I sighed and stared at the poor lame thing. It had caught some kind of fever or been trapped in a germ war and that's about all we knew. It took sick and died inside me and would have taken me with it if it could have. It was just as tormented and sad as could be. I'd miss it, but I wasn't going to act like a man with no guts (ha ha).

Dr. Gorba-something showed me which end was which. He showed me the appendix, dangling there like a little baby. He showed me a piece of the small intestine they'd snipped off for good measure. "In-tes-stein," he said every time.

"Anything else you vant to know?" He had obliged me about as much as I could stand.

"Thanks," I said. "You can throw it away now."

"Oh no," he said, "vee keep zem practically forever. You can come back years from now and see it again. Zey are studied over and over."

So it was to be like an old truck tire. A tire could lie around for a lifetime unless someone poured gasoline on it and burned it. Then it would make one last hoot and holler with black smoke seen all around the countryside.

"Well, whatever." I turned to go. Joe took command of the wheelchair. I knew one thing. I wouldn't be back and I wouldn't be crying over spilt milk.

We were almost out the door when Dr. Gorba-whatever stopped us. "Oh, Mr. Vatkins, one more zing." He stood pointing down at the pan. "You have just seen a perfect example of a cancer host. If zis vere five years later, I vould be showing you your cancerous colon."

That did it. "Joe," I said, once we'd bumped out into the hall, "floorboard this thing. I gotta' get the lead out."

He did, and we didn't hit a single armadillo or turtle on that haul back to the room.

Personal Effects

My two dolls, aged fifty-plus years, are flying away today to the Panhandle for a remodeling job. Every region of Texas has its doll doctor. I trust only the one up on the caprock.

The Betsy Wetsy has had a problem for some time now. She sheds crumbs of foam rubber each time she is touched. It makes loving her hard. So this morning I eviscerate her in the backyard before I pack her. For a moment, she gives me pause, looking at me with those baby doll eyes. When I lay her down to cut her open, her eyes give a sad little click and she sleeps, providing her own anesthesia, her lashes gentle over her still-rosy plaster cheeks.

Before I pack my dolls, I hold each one a little while. The larger one—I know now, didn't when she was my "baby"—is the size of a two-month-old. Her shoeless cracked plaster feet clatter against each other. I might be holding myself—my long-ago child, or my later infant daughter.

I shall miss my dolls in the months they are gone, and it surely will be that long. Something about proximity. They'll be in the world—of course they will be—but they won't be in their rocker in the bedroom corner. They won't be in *my* world.

Like my friend Barbara. I know she's in some world. The pity for me? She's not in *mine*.

I take my dolls to the post office. There in line, I find myself gazing at a stamp poster with the same angel Barbara loved. It's Gabriel, I think, floating sideways, blowing a Christmas trumpet for

157

the United States Postal Service.

Waiting for Barbara to die that day, the final dose of morphine to stop her misery, I wandered into her living room and took from the mantel this same Gabriel, a painted wooden jigsaw version signed with the name of our common friend, a gifted woodworker.

All that long afternoon the angel insisted itself into my hands, pressed to my heart. A half dozen times, I walked from Barbara's bedroom to the mantel, intending to replace it, but I could never give it up.

I hugged it, a mere thing, to me. For Barbara—all I could muster to help her pass through the narrow opening between life and death.

Finally, I took it once again to her room, hardly knowing what I was doing, and this time, on impulse, laid it between her pale feet, spread too far apart for weeks now by the paralysis of her cancer.

Did I want her to walk on that angel like a bridge to heaven? Fly, straddled on the back of it?

I do not know, and even now I'm a little ashamed, as I remember how I stood there at the foot of Barbara's deathbed with what amounted to a doll, unable to take it back, replace it on the shelf, embarrassed to be holding it there between her feet.

Moving up a little in the postal line, I list the objects at home that came from Barbara's hands as gifts: an orange flower pot on which she painted a kneeling Indian woman, a pair of plaster angels snuggling two fine books she also gave me, a clever note pad I cannot bring myself to use. Now, waiting, I gather these up in my mind, name them once more, count them, finger them, all I have left of my friend. They sit benignly, at peace until some day my children clear out the house, claim them for their own.

None of these is Barbara or can ever be. Still, they are imbued with holiness, made magic by her dying. They are not a long way from feathers and bones, bright stones, beads, holy writ.

It is our lot to take what we have, make of it what we will. We are meant to finger the leftovers, rock our old dolls, clutch wooden angels to our breasts.

Later the woodworker would tell me she had intended, for ages, to give Barbara her wooden angel—a pattern Barbara had picked out. With good reasons of her own, our friend was later and later with Barbara's angel, until the last week, not knowing it was the last week, she brought it by, surrendering it to the hospice nurse who met the door. Did I know. . .well, that is, could I tell. . .whether Barbara knew of the gifting?

I think about that angel riding between Barbara's feet, and how, moment after moment unable to take it away, I finally leaned down and, in an act more embarrassing and unexplainable than holding a ten-inch wooden angel to a dying friend's feet, I kissed Barbara's clean cool feet over and over, feet already stepping out across the clouds.

And I know what I must do.

"Oh yes," I tell our friend the woodworker, "oh yes. She knew."

The icons of love. Every sawn figure, book, painted pot, doll. Things that our rough hands must cling to. Clay comforting clay. Brief appearances of a hidden spirit.

Jan Epton Seale, the 2012 Texas Poet Laureate, lives in the Rio Grande Valley of Texas where she writes poetry, essays, and short fiction. Seale is the author of seven books of poetry, two short story collections, three books of nonfiction, and several children's books. She is the recipient of a National Endowment for the Arts fellowship in poetry and seven PEN Syndicated Fiction awards. She is a member of the Texas Institute of Letters.

www.janseale.com

CPSIA information can be obtained at www.ICGtesting.com
Printed in the USA
LVOW12s1410131013

356684LV00002B/117/P

9 780985 255213